KEVIN WATSON / ALEXANDRA YORK

SILVER ROSE ANTHOLOGY

Award-Winning
Short Stories
2001

SILVER ROSE PRESS
an imprint of
ART

AMERICAN RENAISSANCE FOR THE
TWENTY-FIRST CENTURY, INC.
NEW YORK, NY

SILVER ROSE PRESS
an imprint of
ART

AMERICAN RENAISSANCE
FOR THE TWENTY-FIRST CENTURY, INC.
F.D.R. STATION, P.O. BOX 8379, NEW YORK, NY 10150-1919

ART is a 501(c)(3) nonprofit educational foundation dedicated to a
rebirth of beauty and
life-affirming values in all of the fine arts.

Web site: www. ART-21.org
E-mail: ARTinfo@ART-21.org

ISBN 0-9676444-1-0

Book cover design by Kenneth J. Smith, Smith Communications
Silver rose cover drawing by Michael Wilkinson

Copyright Information

—

Table of Contents

Introduction

Short stories are akin to "Once upon a time..." fairytales not in substance, style or fantasy settings but in literary structure. They encapsulate a brief, finite time period and condense their themes by distilling the narrative, dialogue and action to only the essentials. As readers, we need to get to know the characters quickly, be grabbed by the storyline from the outset, experience a satisfying ending and remember a thematic idea. As writers, this is no easy task to fulfill. The art of short story telling is demanding and daunting not only because of its confined length but also because the story adventures and the writing rhythms themselves should be as enjoyable to hear as to read; the form originated, after all, as an oral art.

American Renaissance for the Twenty-first Century (ART) is a 501(c)(3) nonprofit educational foundation with a stated mission to promote a rebirth of beauty and life-affirming values in all of the fine arts. Our award-winning short story choices for this anthology, then, are judged by us to be the best we could find that, along with high technical writing skills, express ART's mission to one degree or another. Out of nearly one thousand stories read and considered from print publications and electronic magazines, twelve were chosen and are presented unedited herein. Silver Rose Anthology readers may be assured in advance that the stories offered within these pages will leave them with fascinating characters to remember and positive ideas to ponder. It is in this uplifting spirit that we commend them to you.

Alexandra York
President, ART
New York City, April, 2002

Preface

In September of 1996, I was invited by Alexandra York to give a reading of one of my short stories in New York City. This was during the American Renaissance for the Twenty-first Century (ART) *Festival of the Arts* presentations. Various readings and performances ran daily in conjunction with the foundation's three-week visual arts exhibit titled THE LEGACY LIVES. The exhibit featured paintings and sculpture from thirty-five of today's finest artists. The collection celebrated "The World at its Most Beautiful and Man and Woman at Their Best." It was an impressive, inspiring and reassuring event. Every work of art expressed high aesthetic beauty as well as deeper positive themes. I was reminded that personal fulfillment is about focusing on that which gives us pleasure and brings meaning to our lives.

Four years later, in the fall of 2000, I suggested that ART undertake a project that would do specifically for my art form what THE LEGACY LIVES exhibit had done for painting and sculpture. I suggested that we find and publish short stories about fictional characters who are living their lives with meaning and purpose, stories that would make us laugh, encourage us to think, and maybe even cause us to reevaluate our own values.

One year later, after the September 11 terrorist attacks on the United States, this idea seemed not only to be timely but actually crucial. Now, more than ever, the world needs art that gives emphasis to life-affirming values, including stories that introduce us to everyday people facing and tackling everyday problems with reason and resolve. I kept this in mind while searching for our award-winning stories.

The Silver Rose is ART's symbol of beauty. The Silver Rose Award for Excellence in the Art of the Short Story was created to honor the writers of exceptional short stories and to draw attention to the publications that bring these fine works to the marketplace. Our "one dozen silver roses" for the year 2001 were culled from large, well-known magazines and from small, lesser-known journals and webzines. And though the writers of these stories all have different voices, their stories strike a similar chord: they speak of the human experience enriched by the struggle for happiness and meaning in life.

It is ART's goal—and mine—to publish a yearly anthology of short stories that challenge thought and evoke emotions, to bring together a collection of short stories about some very special people with whom our readers will enjoy spending their time. I am proud to say that I believe our first Silver Rose Anthology accomplishes this beautifully. I hope you will agree. If so, I encourage you to ensure future collections by sharing these stories with your family and friends.

Kevin Watson
Winston-Salem, NC
April, 2002

Acknowledgements

We wish to thank the members of American Renaissance for the Twenty-first Century foundation for their continuing support, for our members are the strength of our achievements. ART's Board of Directors, Honorary Board and Board of Advisors (volunteers all) are crucial to the leadership of the foundation and we list them here: Directors: Alexandra York, Barrett Randell and Irene Pierpont; Honorary: Joseph Veach Noble and Pierre Rioux; Advisors: EvAngelos Frudakis, Elisabeth Gordon Chandler, Richard Whitney, Samuel Knecht, John Massaro, Frederick Clifford Gibson, Roslyn Targ, William Edward Baer, Gail Dubinbaum, William T. Greene, Diana Brill, Donald Martin Reynolds, Arthur Pontynen, Marc Mellon, Peter Adams and in memoriam Elizabeth de C. Wilson, Rudolph Schirmer and Frederick E. Hart.

We would also like to thank all of the authors whose works are included herein for waiving their reprint fees in honor of the foundation's high mission. This generosity has saved ART several thousand dollars and greatly facilitated the publishing of our first short story anthology. On the other side of that generosity, we are happy to thank certain of ART's members who contributed substantially to this important project with direct donations:

Benefactor ($3,000)
Pierre Rioux
Herrick Jackson & Polly Jackson for The Connemara Fund
Patron ($1,000)
Mr. And Mrs. Floyd Farleigh
Schultz Company
Supporter ($500 or more)
Dollie C. Smith
Pasquale & Shirley Giordano
Michael Wilkinson
Galerie Kornye West

Lastly, we thank Michael Wilkinson for creating and donating his drawing of our symbol of beauty, the Silver Rose, that will appear on all the book covers of our anthology series.

~ xi ~   The Editors

Al Sim
Get The Can
from Glimmer Train Stories

———————————— • ————————————

He was the only haole kid in sight. He was standing in the middle of a tidal channel between the lagoon and the brimless Pacific. They called it Drifter's Reef, but there was no reef out here, just restless green water. He wondered what the Japanese called it when they built the bombed-out causeway he was standing on.

The causeway was made of huge slabs of concrete, stood on edge and bolted together. Narrow gaps a few inches wide separated the slabs. These gaps were filled with water and life. Little day-glo fish swam in the one beneath his feet. He crouched down to get a better look at them. Mike came over and crouched down next to him.

"Pretty neat, yah?" the Japanese-Filipino boy said. "Big schools in da little cracks."

Mike wasn't short for Michael. It was short for Microphone. His father, the air traffic controller, named his first son after the piece of equipment that took him out of the slums of Manila. It actually said "Microphone" on his birth certificate.

The haole boy thought about that while he watched the fish. *His name is Microphone.* The two boys squatted and the little violet and scarlet and electric-orange fish swim beneath their toes.

"See da' one," Mike said.

His finger stretched toward a tiny, pale green fish.

"Poison. Eat it, you die fast."

The haole boy glanced at Mike's dark face to see if it was a lie. He couldn't tell. He looked back at the little fish, but it was gone.

"Why would I eat it?"

The other boy shrugged.

"Mebbe you get hungry."

Mike got to his feet and wandered off down the causeway. The haole boy watched the psychedelic schools of tiny fish for a moment longer, then rose and followed his new friend. They stood at the end of the pitted concrete roadway, where an American bomb had neatly severed it. He looked down at his feet for a moment, at the glass-green water surging past, then followed Mike's gaze up to some older boys on the wooden bridge that paralleled the causeway.

One of them was outside the railing, holding himself up with his arms behind his back. He and the five boys behind him were all peering thirty feet down to the water below.

"What's he doing?" the haole boy asked.

"Gonna ride a ray," Mike said.

He had no idea what Mike meant. Then there was hollering above him, and the boy outside the railing let go and dropped into a dive. The other boys cheered when something happened underwater. Then they fell silent, and what seemed like minutes went by. He thought the boy underwater must surely be drowned. What seemed like more minutes passed. Just as panic started to rise in his throat, the older boy burst out of the sea forty feet away, his fist in the air, yelling victory.

"Come on," Mike said, and they went up on the bridge.

* * *

The bridge was made of heavy timbers treated with creosote. Traffic was almost nonexistent and slow moving. Rusted cars and trucks, ragged holes in their sheet metal eaten by the salty ocean air, rumbled across it at a few miles an hour.

He leaned on the low, thick guardrail and watched the manta rays pass underneath. They were big, silent, slow-motion bats easing from the lagoon out into the deep water, riding the current like hawks on an updraft. He was transfixed.

One of the older boys was Connor Delima, the eldest Delima boy. It was his turn outside the railing. He dove out and dropped into the water, grabbed a ray that looked eight feet wide, and disappeared when it banked down at a sharp angle.

"He betta let go," someone said.

Then they waited. And waited.

"He betta let go," someone else said.

They waited some more. The haole boy stopped breathing. Far too much time passed. The haole boy had to start breathing again.

Then Connor bobbed to the surface what looked like a quarter mile away, almost where the water started to churn as it headed into the open ocean. He yelped once and waved, then went into a crawl and made his way over to the slow water behind the remains of the causeway. A few moments later he scrambled up on the concrete and put his fist in the air.

"He shoulda let go," someone said. "He coulda drown out dere."

Joseph, the second eldest Delima, went down to meet his brother. The others waited. The haole boy tapped Mike on the shoulder.

"You ever do that?" he said.

Mike shook his head.

"Not old enough yet. Not allowed till you thirteen."

Mike turned back to watch the Delima boys approaching each other along the shore.

"Older boys won't let you till you old enough," he said. "Keeps it safe."

Nothing about it seemed safe to the haole boy, and he liked that. He looked down into the water and imagined what it would feel like to ride a big black manta ray, dropping from the bridge into the water, grabbing the strange flat fish, zooming out into the cool green current.

* * *

He was still daydreaming when the two eldest Delima boys came back onto the bridge.

"Any more rays?" Connor said.

A few heads shook.

"Nah," someone said.

The sound of voices brought the haole boy back to the present. Connor sat down on the railing and Joseph sat next to him. A breeze came up and rustled their hair. Little wisps danced on seven dark heads and on one blond one.

"That looks like fun," the haole boy said. "I'd like to try it."

Seven dark heads turned in his direction. Connor broke into a grin. His square white teeth looked like enameled tiles.

"You would, yah? How old you?"

The haole boy looked around. Only Connor was smiling.

"Ten."

Connor nodded.

"Three more years," he said, and looked away.

Mike whispered, *Told you,* in his ear. Connor turned back and his grin was gone.

"You ever play get da can?"

The haole boy hesitated, then shook his head. He didn't understand what the older boy meant. Connor stood up.

"Come on," he said.

* * *

The younger boys followed Connor and Joseph off the bridge. The haole boy asked Mike what was going on.

"Ya gonna play get da can."

"What's that?"

"Throw a can in da wata, wait till it sink, go get it."

The haole boy's heart skipped a beat. Connor and Joseph led them out onto the causeway.

"Connor," Joseph said.

The older boy stopped and turned.

"You got a can?" Joseph asked.

Connor smiled, then pointed at the water on the up-current side of the causeway, where it slowed and pressed against the pitted concrete. He went about ten paces further and dove in. About forty seconds later he came to the surface and tossed a rusted Coke can to his brother.

The can made a rattling, crunching sound. Joseph tilted it to let the water drain and a coral pebble tumbled out. He decreased the angle to keep the other stones from following.

Connor got back up on the concrete and turned to the haole boy.

"Here da rules. I toss da can in da wata, over here where current's not so bad. When bubbles stop, you go get it. Easy, yah?"

The haole boy looked at the water.

"How deep is it?"

Connor shrugged.

"Not too deep. Thirty, forty feet."

Joseph stepped over and stood next to the haole boy. He handed the can to Connor.

"It's about twenty-five feet, maybe a little more," Joseph said. "Connor just wants to scare you."

He spoke in complete sentences and without the pidgin accent. The haole boy looked up at Joseph and studied his face. The non-haole kids spoke that way when they wanted to make him feel better. He almost smiled, then looked back down at the water.

Twenty-five feet, maybe more. Twice as deep as the deepest swimming pool he had ever been in. And full of living things he had never seen the likes of. And with a steady current pushing against the causeway, sucking every loose thing out into the ocean.

"Sure," he said. "That's simple."

Connor grinned at him again, flashed his little rows of bright white squares.

"Why do you wait till the bubbles stop?" the haole boy asked.

"So you can't follow 'em down," Joseph answered.

"Why don't you fill the can with water so it doesn't leave any bubbles?"

Joseph looked at his brother.

"This one thinks of everything."

Connor grinned again. Joseph explained.

"With water in it, the can goes straight down. It's too easy to find. Air makes it skip around a little, because it floats some. It doesn't go straight down."

The haole boy nodded.

"Sure," he said. "Makes sense."

He stared into the water.

"You want me to go first?" Joseph asked.

The haole boy glanced up at him, then looked at Connor's blank face. He turned back to Joseph.

"No," he said.

Joseph patted the haole boy's shoulder, then took a few steps away and stood near his older brother. Connor spoke to the haole boy.

"When I say go, okay?"

The haole boy was staring into the water again.

"Okay?" Connor repeated.

The haole boy snapped his head around.

"Sure," he said.

Connor flipped the Coke can into the water. The haole boy moved to the edge of the concrete and stood in a slight crouch. Eight boys waited in silence, eyes on the small stream of bubbles. They fizzled and stopped. A moment passed.

"Go," Connor said.

* * *

The haole boy jumped almost straight up, and dove almost straight down. He went about five feet under without a stroke. Down below him, the can had tilted slightly, and a last few bubbles had slipped out. He saw the little flashes of silver emerge from the opaque layer below and he swam toward them.

The water grew colder and greener and his chest felt heavy. He saw dark forms swimming away from him, nothing too big, probably the outer fringes of a school of mullet. He couldn't help hoping that a ray would come along and he could grab a ride.

Another silver flash, below and a little to his left, and he changed course. Then he could see a glimpse of red, and he swam toward that. He lost it in the murk, but kept going and it emerged again.

He found the Coke can standing upright on a seaweed-covered block of concrete from the bombed-out causeway. The concrete chunk was about the size and shape of a steamer trunk. The seaweed billowed in the current, tendrils about three feet long rising up around the can. His heart throbbed as he swam close and reached in among the waving fronds, clutched the can, and turned to the surface.

He paused when he saw it, high above him, a rippling greenish-silver ceiling. It looked too far away, too far to go. He watched it shimmer and undulate like spilled mercury, and somehow it came closer and grew softer.

He wondered if Mike and Joseph were worried he would drown. Part of him wanted to stay down there, watching the surface shimmer and ripple, and wait to see how long it would take before someone came in after him.

He let a few bubbles slide out of his mouth and watched them wobble and rise. Then he gave a sharp kick and let the big bubble in his chest carry him upward. The rusted can felt perfect in his tight little hand.

* * *

Al Sim turned eight on Wake Island, a coral atoll 1,800 miles west of Hawaii. Get the Can *won the 2001 Glimmer Train Stories Very Short Fiction Award. His stories have appeared in a number of publications, including* Thin Air, Crab Creek Review, *and* Red Cedar Review. *Stories are forthcoming in the* Raven Chronicles *and the* Literary Review. *He is currently writing a novel.*

Robert Olen Butler

Rafferty And Josephine

from Zoetrope: All-Story

———————•———————

Josephine Claiborne paused, her hands hanging over the keyboard, as her lovely vampire heroine, Marie Therese, first laid eyes on the handsome Union captain she would love and devour. Josephine was suddenly conscious of her own body. Knowing what her character must inevitably do to protect herself, to nourish herself, she had grown breathless. Her lips tingled. She bared her teeth. This stopped her. I'm getting a little too much into this, she thought, and she turned to look at her Writing Tree, a great, gnarled live oak just outside her window. Through the lift of its dark arms she could see a gaggle of tourists on St. Charles Avenue, their faces raised to her window, ropes of beads around their necks, and beside them, pointing through the tree at the great lady at work, was Delphine. Josephine was surprised that her daughter was conducting the literary tour herself today, though it no doubt had to do with shorthandedness during Mardi Gras. Delphine had written the script of the tour, and Josephine knew it by heart, so she could read her daughter's lips: "This is where Josephine Claiborne lives alone, weaving her dark tales of love and death from the well of her own solitude."

Josephine growled at this—at the sentiment and at Delphine's penchant for mixing metaphors—and she looked back to the computer and she tried to focus on her own words again. Then her hands dashed on. The Union captain took Marie Therese in his arms and they waltzed out the balcony doors and into the hot Louisiana night.

A chorus of voices arose from the street. "Bring your face close!" they cried. Josephine lifted her hands and turned back to the window. This was her cue. The phrase was her signature, slipped into every book. She wiggled her fingers at the benighted Union captain, wishing to go on without stopping, but she'd promised Delphine always to make an appearance when she heard these words, and so she rose and lifted the window and Delphine waved and Josephine waved back and the tourists cheered.

"We love you, Josephine!" one cried, and the others took it up.

"More than Anne Rice?" Josephine called, and she could sense Delphine's disapproval, though her smile stayed fixed on her face.

"Yes!" they replied as one.

Josephine was supposed to say something nice now. *I love you, too.* Or, *You're all too wonderful.* She was glad they loved her more than anyone, but she was pissed at this interruption and so she merely waved and cried, "Buy my books!"

"We will!"

The unflappable good nature of these literary tourists softened Josephine. She regretted her grumpiness. So she gave them a double dose of Delphine's script, softening her voice as much as she could and still be heard: "I love you, too! You're all too wonderful!"

Josephine drew back in. She hunched over the keyboard with the flounce of a concert pianist and she read the passage on the screen before her. "You're all too wonderful," Josephine whispered to the words she'd just written.

* * *

Meanwhile, down St. Charles and across Canal Street and in the midst of the welter of the long Mardi Gras weekend in the French Quarter, at a table for two next to a window on Chartres, the most desired lunchtime table in arguably one of the three best restaurants in all the Vieux Carré, if not all New Orleans, namely Rafferty's—though there was a bit more than a touch of resentment from some of the old guard that a restaurateur who made his mostly cultish reputation in a ramshackle, lunch—only seafood place in the Ninth Ward would dare to cross Canal and insinuate himself onto Chartres, even within sight of Jackson Square— at this table for two sat Rafferty himself, Rafferty McCue, with the curtains drawn beside him and his restaurant empty and its lacework iron door locked and a sign upon it reading "Gone to Mardi Gras, bring your appetites with your ashen foreheads on Wednesday." He watched shadows of the revelers dancing on the curtains like a Balinese puppet show and he wanted to be content where he was, alone at this table, though he was beginning to think Aspen would be a better place, with most of the other uptown New Orleanians who opted out of the krewes and the balls.

Max sat down opposite him with a rustling of paper.

A great shadow headdress had appeared on the curtain and stopped and quaked there, and it struck Rafferty as quite wonderfully feminine in its feathery roundness. For the past few years, as his widowerhood had become a habit, he'd grown intensely conscious of feminine things.

"Dad, you need to read this."

Rafferty turned to Max, who was waving a stack of contracts at him. Perhaps Rafferty was showing his mood on his face, because his son took one look and amended his order: "Or just sign."

Though Rafferty had only recently slipped past fifty, he was more interested these days in choosing the pompano or stirring the roux or shaking every hand at every table in the place than he was in the things his Harvard-M.B.A. son was only too happy to handle. "I'll sign," he said.

The contracts were before him, Max flipping the pages to the red-arrow tabs. Rafferty started signing. "We're ready to do more, right?"

"You're not getting cold feet." Max's voice had turned suddenly brittle.

Rafferty raised his eyes to his son.

"It's a *great* property," Max said. "The best double-gallery house on Magazine Street. It's big and it's ready for the Poland Avenue treatment."

Rafferty focused on the next dotted line.

"I don't want to make you do something you feel is a mistake," Max said.

Rafferty didn't think this was strictly true. He lifted his pen in mid-signature and looked up, not knowing whether to be irritated or playful. Either way, he'd say the same thing, so he said it: "Is that true?" As Rafferty expected, his son's eyes widened ever so slightly in panic.

"This isn't a mistake," Max said, a little breathless.

"But if I *thought* it was a mistake, you wouldn't want to make me do it?"

"If you thought it was a mistake but it wasn't?"

"Yes."

Rafferty could see Max trying to decide whether to lie or not.

Max chose a middle path. "Well," he said, "maybe I'd want to make you do it."

"But you wouldn't try."

Max looked abruptly away and down, as if a small boy had suddenly tugged at his sleeve. "OK, Dad," he said to the floor, and then he looked back at Rafferty. "You're right. No more bullshit. I want you to do this no matter what you think about it."

Father and son looked at each other calmly, no bullshit between them for the moment, and then Rafferty gave Max a slow, warm smile. "I trust you, Max," Rafferty said, and he meant it. Even while Max was at Harvard, he'd revived the Poland Avenue location, which was rooted in Rafferty's personal history and which almost faded away when he'd brought the family recipes to the Quarter. Max had done it with lots of neon and a Cajun band and a TV ad with Rafferty in a Saints uniform throwing a jumbo shrimp, like a sidelines pass, into Mike Ditka's mouth. Now the tourists actually came to the Ninth Ward to eat fried green tomatoes and oyster shooters and Redfish Rafferty elbow to elbow with Harry Connick Jr. or Anne Rice or Dr. John or even Edwin Edwards taking a lunch break from Harrah's or his latest trial. So if Max could be manipulative at times, a bit of a patronizing prick, that was probably part of being a top-tier M.B.A. "It's your baby," Rafferty said to his son.

Max reached out and briefly squeezed his father's forearm. A beat later he nodded at the idle pen.

* * *

Max had already prepared for the contract signing: news of the purchase was in the next morning's *Times Picayune*. Rafferty sat on his wraparound porch having coffee with chicory and he lowered his paper and humphed softly, mostly in appreciation of his son's initiative, though if Max had been there, Rafferty would have ragged him for his presumption. He lifted the paper again while a mile down St. Charles Avenue there was, prompted by the very same news story, a sudden sharp yawp on Josephine Claiborne's breakfast veranda. Delphine, who was the yawper, also jumped to her feet and Josephine sloshed her own coffee with chicory into its saucer. "What is it?" Josephine cried, fearing fire ants.

"They've grabbed the LeBlanc House."

Josephine thought of terrorists. "Why on earth . . . ?"

"They want to string it with neon lights and fill it with whorehouse plush."

Josephine tried to figure out whose radical political agenda was that tacky.

After a moment, Delphine realized she wasn't getting through to her mother. She said, "Those people who own the Rafferty's restaurants. They've just bought LeBlanc House." Delphine collapsed back into her wicker chair.

"They'll destroy it with light and noise and bad taste. They'll defile *Voodoo Vampire*."

Though it was early in the morning and though Josephine's novelist's mind wanted to linger with the alternate story of tacky terrorists on Magazine Street, she put her coffee down and, perhaps from the ongoing dream of her new novel, she felt as if she wanted to bite something. *Voodoo Vampire* had been her first big bestseller and the LeBlanc House was the setting for the novel's grand ball scene.

"It's easily one of the three or four most popular spots on the tour," Delphine said.

Josephine waited for more. But Delphine grumped under her breath and sighed and then returned to her coffee.

"So?" Josephine said. Something was suddenly nibbling around in her, a prickly little pain.

"I'll change the script."

Josephine waited again. Delphine handled Josephine's press and publicity, but her public relations firm was much more than Josephine Claiborne now. It was a microbrewery, a senatorial candidate, the Association of New Orleans Street Performers, Bayou Viagra Hot Sauce, and more and more all the time. Josephine understood the nibbling even as it grew fiercer. She felt neglected by her own daughter. She felt jealous. She was ashamed of these feelings but it didn't stop her from saying, "That's it? What was that whole leap-in-the-air-and-shout thing about?"

"I'm damn angry." She sipped her coffee.

"This is something I never noticed before," Josephine said. "That a surge of anger has this languor afterward, like after sex."

Delphine narrowed her eyes, trying to figure out the rebuke.

"Darling, you sent me around in a coffin for the *Voodoo Vampire* book tour. What's happened to your initiative? They defile my vampire space and you go back to your coffee?"

Delphine looked at the cup in her hand.

Josephine silently upbraided herself. Stop this right now. There's nothing to be done about the LeBlanc House. More important, Delphine deserves her own life away from you. And she said, "Isn't there something?"

Delphine jumped up again. "You're right, Mama. Let's kick their ass."

"Go for the jugular, sweetie," Josephine said, feeling shamefully pleased at her daughter's attention.

* * *

On the night of this day there was a masked charity ball in a great ballroom in a Vieux Carré hotel with a bar named Desire, and Rafferty put on a black cloak and the mask of Mephisto, and Josephine put on a bouffant satin gown with an overskirt of chiffon starry-skied with rhinestones and a sweetheart bodice of brocade fruited with silver fringe pearls, aurora borealis stones, sequins, and bugle beads, and she wore the mask of a princess, the very face she imagined for Marie Therese DeSang. The room swirled with waltzing princes and pirates and whores and goddesses and gods and sailors, and beneath the churn of violins and the deep thump of percussion was the soft clash of bangles and chains and plumes and trailings of fur and silk and feathers, and the dancers swooped and spun and others of their kind crowded close watching or leaning together or swaying or bending to press their words through the music, and all the eyes in these faces of porcelain or canvas or leather or felt were wide and fixed and the brows neither rose nor fell and the cheeks were high and rouged red, and the only unmasked faces in the place were fixed, too, as chins clutched violins and eyes closed and bows swooped and fell and swooped to the dark flow of the Masquerade Waltz and near the orchestra an Aztec sun king who had once tasted true absinthe was briefly transported by the thought of his mother waltzing with him, many years ago, and he spilled his Pernod on the goddess Mnemosyne who backed abruptly into Joan of Arc in full armor who lurched into the path of a high-hatted lawyer and his creole mistress whose crinolines deflected them and in so doing moved another couple and another and the eddy of dancers reshaped along the floor until Shakespeare swung his Dido into a tuxedoed waiter in a jester mask whose lifted tray tipped from his fingers and fried oysters tumbled down Eurydice's chest and into her cleavage and she invoked the hell where her well-meaning but stupid husband had stranded her and he himself who was dressed this year as an Indian chief lifted his tomahawk as if to have the scalp of the waiter but in fact he only jostled the passing Mephisto just enough to bend his path into a turning princess and so it was that Rafferty and Josephine collided.

"I beg your pardon," Rafferty said and he lifted her hand and bent to it and placed the mouth of his mask there and the gesture had come from the music and the glitter of this princess and he held his face there, unable, of course, to work the lips into the appropriate action. Rafferty and Josephine held the pose for a moment, she waiting, he contemplating what it was he was doing, and then he said, "Kiss kiss," and rose from her hand with a flourish of his cape. They looked at each other, mask to mask.

"Blush blush," Josephine said.

"Flirt flirt," Rafferty said.

"Ah, but how, precisely? You've gone quite vague."

"Wink wink, then."

"Good. Blush blush eye-flutter eye-flutter."

"Wink wink brow-wiggle brow-wiggle leer leer."

Josephine cocked her head at this man. "Please. I expected better than a leer, even from the devil himself."

"The devil is much more mundane than anyone suspects," Rafferty said.

"Perhaps you're right. Certainly this Southern belle is quite different from what you'd expect. Leer away then. I must make do."

And they stood before each other, having riffed together,

instinctively, in a way that had been rare for each of them but which felt very good here with the music and the welter of strangers around them, and Rafferty said, "Are you free to waltz?"

"I am."

And they took each other in their arms and slid into the flow of dancers and his cape billowed and her rhinestones glittered, and mask before mask they danced spinning beneath a great chandelier and past first Amelia Earhart in flying togs and then, a brief time later, past King Louis the Fourteenth in a golden robe and both Amelia and Louis turned to look, and Josephine and Rafferty whirled on before the orchestra and each was thinking, *I know nothing of this body holding mine he could be half my age she could be ugly*, and they spun on, their feet moving lightly, synchronized as if they had done this for years together, and they quickly concluded that they'd thought wrong, *I am agelessly sexy I care nothing of her looks if she has this wit*, and Rafferty said, "Are you alone?"

"No." And Josephine knew he meant, *Are you with a man*, but she hesitated a beat onetwothree and another onetwothree and she wished to see the face behind his mask to see if his misimpression mattered to him but she could not and then onetwothree she said, "I'm here with my daughter."

"And I'm with my son."

"I'm smiling," she said.

"So am I," he said.

"Why?" The question flew from her of its own will and they spun on.

"We are so far only masks to each other," he said, elaborating on her question, revealing to her, actually, what she'd just meant, and this made her smile again, though she did not say so.

"And quite incompatible masks," she said.

"Do you think?"

"Are you not the very devil himself, sir?"

"Is your princess incorruptible?"

"God no. She has fangs."

They danced on not speaking further, their feet never missing a step onetwothree and Amelia Earhart looked again and though her fixed, famous face did not show it, the look was intense, and Josephine caught a glimpse and she said, "That's my daughter we just passed. Amelia Earhart," and Rafferty turned his face to see and Amelia was gone but there was a great golden robe and another face intent upon the couple and Rafferty said, "That's my son Louis the Fourteenth."

"Your son was once very unkind to one of my characters."

They swirled past the orchestra with Rafferty silently trying to figure this out and Josephine realizing she was very pleasantly awaiting whatever it was this man would say next. Then she understood his hesitation. "Your son *Louis*," she said. "He banished her to Louisiana before there was a New Orleans, though she wreaked a terrible revenge. She was a character in one of my books. I'm a writer."

Rafferty instantly picked up where he'd broken off. "He must have had a good reason. To banish her."

"Please," Josephine said, "I should know."

"Forgive me. He is my son."

"He is grown. You can't protect him forever."

"Should I speak to you honestly then of your daughter's overrated flying skills?"

And the music quickly built to a crescendo and stopped. Rafferty and Josephine stopped, too, but they did not let go of each other. They found themselves in the same place: wishing for music, not wanting to let go, wearying of their own arch indirectness.

Rafferty said, "Would you like to step outside of this room?"

She would and they did, he taking her hand and leading the way through the crowd and both of them feeling the fleshy immediacy of the touch of a new hand and wondering what was happening. Then, in the corridor outside the ballroom, with a new waltz muffling into life behind the closed doors and with the brightness of the light here, the both of them, without thinking, lifted their hands to their masks and with a faint quaking inside, as if they were two new lovers rendering themselves naked together for the first time, they stripped off their masks.

Though it was not uncommon in Josephine's novels for her heroine to suck the blood of any man who was interested in her, nevertheless taking great sensual pleasure in the act—the foundation of her wide popularity with modern women—and though she considered herself a true writer, expressing her own personal view of the world in her work, she found that this man's face pleased her inordinately, the boyish cheek-pinchiness of it, and she felt a serious warm fluttery thing beginning in her, and she didn't want to suck his blood at all, merely nibble on his earlobes perhaps. What did this response betoken in her? She declined to answer as she stood naked-faced before this man who was even then feeling a similarly tender thing, the habit of Rafferty's aloneness falling away at once before this woman's lovely thin-nosed high-browed face with the tracings of a rich life of the senses around her eyes and mouth. He wanted to take her in his arms once more, and it was Mardi Gras, after all, it was New Orleans, after all—he wanted to kiss her. Rafferty and Josephine stood sweetly suspended like this for a long moment and before either of them could move or even speak, the music surged loud from the direction of the ballroom and Rafferty's eyes shifted just slightly to see Amelia Earhart emerge and then stagger at the sight of him. She revved her engines and buzzed the field.

"You're Rafferty McCue," Amelia said. "We're going to sue your ass."

* * *

Things had gone quickly bad from there, as Louis the Fourteenth appeared in the corridor soon after, and if there had been swords to draw, they would have been drawn, and Rafferty and Josephine seemed to lose the power of speech as Amelia Earhart and King Louis debated, in a condensed and strident form, the trade-offs of history and commercial progress, of intellectual rights and property rights, of good taste and bad, of his arrogantly patronizing tone and her strident hysteria. And then finally Delphine stripped off her mask and said, "Mama, let's go. We'll fight these people till the bitter end," and her adversary stripped off his mask, revealing a face that Josephine found herself feeling instantly kindly toward, for it had the same blue flash of eyes and baby-bottom cheeks of the man she'd just danced with. Then Delphine's hand was under Josephine's elbow and they were moving away and Josephine barely had time to glance back, and she and Rafferty shared a last look, wistful in its blankness.

Josephine tried to force her mind away from the whole incident as she lay that night in her bed and listened to distant laughter and the faint pop of a faraway firecracker. The irony was not lost on Josephine: her stirring up her daughter against the man with whom she would, that very night, dance, and dance quite wonderfully. And Desiree Jones waltzed into Josephine's mind, Desiree the beautiful octaroon orphan of *Voodoo Vampire*, reared as the daughter of the great Voodoo Priestess, Lily DeSang. Early in the book, Desiree had fallen in love with a dashing white New Orleans lawyer, the wealthy Marcellus Breckinridge, and though, as a result, she had incurred the frightening rage and the formidable threats of her Voodoo mother, she left DeSang and became Breckinridge's mistress. Now the two of them were dancing, Desiree and Marcellus, in the second-floor ballroom of the disputed LeBlanc House and the words were clear in Josephine's head, she'd risen from her traveling coffin in forty-five bookstores across America and read: *Desiree danced with her heart whirling faster than her body. She was in his arms; she belonged to him alone at last. And then, even as he lifted her up in a grand spin, her gaze fell upon the window and there she was. The face was unmistakable and ghastly in the light from the great chandelier. It was Lily DeSang. Desiree tried to resist these eyes. But they were the eyes of the only mother she'd ever known. And she drew Marcellus to a stop and she excused herself and she headed for the balcony door.*

"Don't go," Josephine whispered into the dark. But Desiree did not stop. She moved to the door and out into the night.

Lily was before her, quickly, gliding across the balcony, and Desiree wanted to stand up to her, wanted to tell her she loved her but it was time to find a life of her own. She did not have a chance. Lily put her arms around Desiree and for a moment it seemed that everything was going to be all right, her mother would understand. Then Lily bent near and Desiree felt the two points of pain flare in the side of her neck and a terrible coldness came over her and a weakness and she knew she would always be the darkly dutiful daughter of Lily DeSang and there was a knock at the door. Josephine started and sat up.

"Mama?" It was Delphine's voice. She was staying the night in her room in Josephine's house, avoiding the Mardi Gras madness in the Quarter. "Are you awake?" she asked, low.

"Yes, dear. Come in."

Delphine slipped into the room and sat on the edge of Josephine's bed. "We haven't talked yet about . . . you know."

"The devil."

"And his minion."

"I didn't even know who he was until you arrived. That was Rafferty McCue, you say?"

"The *restaurant owner*," Delphine said, her emphasis making it sound like *car thief*. "From the *Ninth Ward*," she added, which sounded even worse. "I'll drive him off Magazine Street. Believe me."

This was what Josephine had kindled in her daughter. She felt suddenly like Lily DeSang, after having bitten her daughter in the throat and shaped her to her own dark will. But how could she undo it? And did she really want to? Josephine hardly knew this man. He was a fetching face, some sweet banter.

"Why doesn't he leave you alone?" Delphine said.

"We only danced."

"Your landmark."

"I didn't know."

"These people are bad news," Delphine said, patting Josephine on the hand as if she were the mother. "Thanks for the pep talk this morning. You're still my top client." Delphine rose and headed for the door.

Josephine tried to balance the little she had of Rafferty against the weight of her work, her legend, the renewed vigor of her daughter's allegiance. Delphine's hand was on the doorknob and she turned to her mother. Josephine jumped up and crossed to her, saying, "Hug hug." The phrase surprised both of them. Cutesy talk had been banned between them before Delphine even had breasts. But Josephine knew where that talk had come from. And Delphine complied, squaring around and offering her torso. Josephine hugged her and found, to her surprise, that she wished she could take back the bite.

* * *

At the same moment, in the bar named Desire, Rafferty and Max sat at a corner table in robe and cloak, their evening's faces propped side by side against the wall behind the salt and pepper shakers, and Max said, "Did you know?"

"She said she was a writer. That's as far as I got before the shit hit Amelia Earhart's propeller."

"I'm sure that's where she was heading."

"Who?"

"Josephine Claiborne."

"Heading where, exactly?"

Max puffed in exasperation at his father. "Getting you to back off from the LeBlanc House."

"It seemed to be the daughter's beef."

"It's the *mother's* holy ground we're trampling on."

Rafferty sagged inside. He didn't wonder why. The face of this Josephine Claiborne floated still in his head, sweeter to him than the princess in her mask. But Max was smart in these things. The woman who'd awakened him was merely after something. Then a thought lifted him. "Wait a minute," he said. "There was no way for her to know it was me."

"There's no basis for a suit," Max said. "That's crazy."

"I didn't have my mask off all night. Not till . . ."

"Dad. That's not the basic point. Lawsuit or not, they can make things nasty for us. She's got a lot of power in this town, power with the people. PR." Max paused and leaned across the table. "*We want this restaurant.*"

This last was said with more passion than Rafferty had heard in his son's voice in a long time. Max missed his mother badly. After her death, he'd trimmed his feelings back as neatly as the ivy on Harvard's walls. The LeBlanc House seemed to be changing all that. Rafferty heard the neon in his son's voice and he was grateful for that. And yet he could not hold Max's bright eyes before him. His gaze turned inward where all he could see was Josephine's face emerging, luminously naked, from behind its mask.

* * *

Rafferty spent the next day hiding in the little office off his kitchen on Chartres Street. Max was somewhere with his girlfriend, who was a lawyer, and it was impossible to guess whether they were partying or going over contracts, and Rafferty closed his door and even the tempest of Mardi Gras felt far away. He threw himself into the restaurant paperwork and he studied the menu, trying to see the culinary gaps, and he left his confinement only to scramble himself some eggs with onions and Tabasco sometime in the middle of the day. It was late when he finally pushed back from his desk and stared at the ceiling and let himself actually think about the question that had been running in him all day: What was there to do about this woman?

Forget her, was one answer.

He tried that one by sliding back under his desk and groping around and finding the menu and looking at it one more time. This restaurant and the one on Poland Avenue and—yes—the new one that was springing from his dear and only son's mind and talents on Magazine Street: these were his life at fifty. These were his work and his identity and they were the bond with what was left of his family. But his eyes fell on an appetizer—one he did especially well—and he felt itchy with the desire to spear an Oyster Bienville on a tiny fork and place it on Josephine Claiborne's tongue.

What was another answer? Talk to her. Try to see her.

His hands, eager and naïve as they were, went at once to the phone book, though Rafferty didn't hold out much hope for the quest. A woman of her fame would never be listed. But his hands worked on and his forefinger went down the Claibornes and there she was: Josephine Claiborne. The hands were vindicated and they charged on, picking up the phone and dialing the number, though Rafferty was fluttery with trepidation.

A recorded message answered at once. He recognized Josephine's voice. "Hello," it said. "This is Josephine Claiborne. You've reached my special fan hot line. I'm busy at work on a brand-new book . . ." and she went on to talk about the Civil War and the beautiful Southern belle who was in fact a vampire using her dark powers to try to defend the Confederacy and find eternal love, as well. But Rafferty wasn't absorbing much. He was caught by the sheer sound of her, by the thought of her lips shaping words. Then she was saying, "If you'd like to leave me a message, you can speak after the beep. And thank you so much for reading my books."

Rafferty felt a clutching in his throat as he waited for

the beep, his hands, still dreaming of placing an oyster on her tongue, not letting him hang up.

* * *

In the house with the machine that was about to sound its beep, Josephine had been acting out a day similar to Rafferty's. She closed the door of her writing room and closed the shades, even to her Writing Tree—she was not superstitious; she could find words on her own— and she fired up her computer and Marie Therese was there for her at once and the words flowed and flowed and finally Marie Therese was ready to bite her love and bring him into the Dark Forever of her own life and Josephine stopped. She was, herself, breathing heavily. But she was no longer inside Marie Therese. She was Josephine. And Josephine's lips trilled with the yearning to kiss a man she knew not to kiss.

She turned away from her computer. And she saw the light on the answering machine beside her reading chair. A fan was calling. She could use the adulatory distraction of a fan right now. Delphine had made her promise when the fan hot line was installed to pick up the phone occasionally and talk to whoever was there. It was good public relations. And right now it seemed very good therapy. So she rose and went to her chair and sat and she reached out and then hesitated, even as the machine was about to offer her fan a beep. She beat the tone by only a second, lifting the handset and putting it to her ear and saying, "Hello?"

On the other end, Rafferty made an incoherent sound from surprise and nervousness and desire, though all of this hardly registered on Josephine. She simply had the impression that someone was choking, though quite softly.

"Are you there?" Josephine said. "This is Josephine. Not the machine. I'd be happy to take your message personally."

Nothing.

"Are you all right? Are you choking?" she asked, though now there was only silence.

"I'm sorry," Rafferty said. "You took me by surprise."

"It's you," she said.

"I hope you mean Rafferty."

"I do."

"I'm sorry. I was going to leave this Josephine Claiborne the novelist a little message."

"Go ahead," Josephine said, quite softly.

Rafferty started choking again.

"Would you like me to beep for you?" Josephine asked.

"It wouldn't do any good. You've called my bluff."

"You have nothing to say to me?"

"Just . . ." Rafferty struggled to figure out what exactly he wanted here. Then he knew. "Just that I'd like to see you sometime. Without a mask and without historical figures nearby to put us at odds."

"Those weren't historical figures," Josephine said. "Those were our children."

"Yes," Rafferty said. "You're right. The children we love and are devoted to."

"Yes."

"And who would control us, if they could?" Rafferty crimped up the end of his sentence to make it a question. He was thinking of Max. He didn't know about this woman's daughter.

"Or we, them." Josephine thought of herself and Delphine, but wondered if it was Rafferty himself who loved neon and whorehouse plush and, if he did, how they'd ever decorate a room together.

The two fell silent again. Finally Josephine said, "When?"

"I'm an impatient man."

"Tomorrow then."

"Fat Tuesday," Rafferty said.

"We should be discreet."

"I think I know a place."

* * *

A stingray glided by, directly over Rafferty's head, and then a porcupine puffer as big as a fire hydrant. Rafferty stood in the center of the underwater tunnel of the Aquarium of the Americas, surrounded by half a million gallons of water. As he'd expected, the place was nearly empty, with the revelry building to a climax just a few blocks away. He lowered his face and half a dozen bright silver Mexican lookdowns, their mouths drawn into frowns, slid by, their bodies suddenly turning into knife blades, nearly vanishing, as they wheeled around and faced him head-on. "Hello, girls," he said, their thin elegance reminding him of fashion models.

"Do you often talk to fish?"

He turned. It was Josephine.

He smiled. "While I was waiting I confessed to a monkfish."

"What was your sin? Buying the LeBlanc House?"

"I thought we'd leave that for a while."

"Yes," Josephine said. "I'm sorry."

They watched a little flurry of coming and going before them—a parrotfish, then a royal gramma and a queen trigger, then the lookdowns reappeared, gliding past. Josephine said,

"Aren't those the girls?"

"Yes they are."

"They're very skinny."

"Yes they are."

"Is that what attracts you to them?" Josephine asked.

Rafferty knew she was joking, but he also knew enough to take a little leap with her. He looked at her until she turned her face to him and he said, "You are quite wonderfully slender."

Josephine's eyebrows lifted and then she smiled. She found she liked being caught off balance by this man. She said, "You do know what a girl wants to hear."

Rafferty put on a very serious face. "Right. 'You're skinny' and 'I'd just as soon cuddle.'"

Josephine laughed, lifting her head back to do so and exposing her throat, which seemed to Rafferty as kissable as her lips. When she stopped laughing and was looking again at him, something more serious had come over her. She said, "Do we talk too cute sometimes?"

"We haven't had enough *times* yet in order to even have a *sometimes*," Rafferty said and he regretted answering her serious question with more cuteness.

"Wow," Josephine said. "That's true, isn't it."

The shadow of some great fish passed over them, but they did not look up. They studied each other's eyes for a long moment and finally Rafferty said, "It's pretty much life-story time, isn't it."

"I think so," Josephine said.

And so they walked among fish and spoke of things that were relevant and irrelevant to the present moment and it was impossible to tell these two kinds of things apart. Rafferty grew up in the Irish Channel and his father was a policeman, but Rafferty preferred his mother's kitchen and he learned to cook, much to the dismay of his father, and after high school he started in the kitchen at Brennan's and he kept his eyes and ears open and then, with the help of some independent money his mother had—and which he paid back, at his insistence, with loan shark's interest—he started a restaurant on Poland Avenue, and he called it Rafferty's. He married a fellow kitchen worker from Brennan's and she had died three years ago after fighting ovarian cancer for longer than anyone figured she would and they had one child, Max, who had his mother's eyes and her mix of practical good sense and bullheadedness and, yes, manipulativeness.

Josephine grew up in the house she now lived in and the

Claiborne of Claiborne Avenue was a distant uncle, and her father was wealthy from oil and her mother was wealthy from her father's oil and Josephine went off to Vanderbilt and she married by reflex upon graduation, when the only life she had imagined for herself was being married, and a mere six months before an acrimonious divorce, her only child came of that marriage, Delphine, who thankfully bore nothing recognizable of her father and who studied English literature at Radcliffe and started her own public relations firm, which took Josephine as its first client.

Josephine had always written. She was an only child and perhaps that had something to do with it. She always wrote stories, telling the things to the paper that she otherwise would have told to her sisters in their beds in the dark, especially in the dead quiet dark when Fat Tuesday had turned into Ash Wednesday, when the thrilling blare of Mardi Gras had suddenly turned into silence. That was a night when she'd always stayed awake to write the stories she yearned to speak.

And after speaking all of this, Rafferty and Josephine themselves fell into silence as they sat before a tank of jellyfish. Rafferty's mind tracked through Josephine's story and came to a thing that Rafferty spoke almost to himself. "That's tonight," he said.

Josephine shook off her own meditation on Rafferty's life. "What?"

"The night of the year that made you a writer. It's tonight."

Josephine liked the way he spun what she'd said. "Yes. It did do that."

Rafferty watched a great moonjelly throb its way upward in the tank. After a moment Josephine said, "Was your wife witty?"

"Yes." Rafferty thought he sensed a flinch in Josephine. He added softly, "I'm not seeing her in you."

Josephine didn't realize that this was the little stutter in her until Rafferty said it. Somewhat to her surprise she felt a twist of resentment at that, as if he'd abruptly put his hand on her breast, although, also to her surprise, that's where her breast presently wanted his hand. She looked away. "Yow," she said.

"Yow?" Rafferty asked.

"Yow," Josephine said, knowing instantly she could not find a way even to begin to explain.

"I see," said Rafferty, and he sort of did see the part about his knowing what she was feeling. "And your husband. Do I remind you of him?"

"If you did, we wouldn't be sitting here."

Rafferty found that this pleased him very much. He was prepared to be retrospectively jealous of the man. He wondered if he should tell her as much, but he decided against it. That was surely near the top of the list of things a girl does *not* want to hear. He regretted now even bringing it up, for he could feel Josephine pulling into herself. "We've had a little too much life-story time," he said.

"I think you're right."

"At least it brought us to this moment," Rafferty said. The words suddenly sounded glib to him. He checked to see if he meant them. He did.

Josephine might have wondered about his sincerity as well, but he'd done it again, spoken truly a thing she herself was feeling. "And it gave us the children we're proud of," she said, and upon hearing her own words she checked to see if her devotion to Delphine would destroy what was happening with this man. She did not know.

A brooding silence came upon them both and finally Josephine said, "I should go."

"All right," Rafferty said, something that seemed like panic rising in his chest like a jellyfish. He added, trying not to sound desperate, "But I didn't even get a chance to buy you a cup of coffee."

It was all on Josephine now. All she needed to say was, I don't think that would be a good idea, or even, some other time, and they could go straight to the place where part of her feared they were inevitably heading. And yet, she said, "Tomorrow."

"Yes?" Rafferty said, though it felt more like a gasp to him.

"Another thing I've always loved is Jackson Square on Ash Wednesday. It's like those hours in the dark."

"I'll meet you there at noon," Rafferty said.

* * *

When Josephine arrived at her house, the sidewalks and neutral ground along St. Charles were awash with Mardi Gras trash, but the crowds were mostly gone, having migrated downtown. There was a message on Josephine's private answering machine. Delphine said, "Mama, I thought you were going to wave at the Rex parade from your window. I had a photographer ready." There was one beat of silence, then another, as Delphine apparently reviewed her tone of voice, which clearly sounded miffed. She softened only a little bit. "I need to talk with you about this whole LeBlanc House thing. Earl says there's really nothing we can do in the courts. But don't worry. I'm going to carry the ball, Mama, and they're not getting off the hook. Call me on the cell. Bye."

Josephine's hand went to the phone, but then pulled back. Who taught her to use language that way? she wondered. Josephine felt as if she herself were on the hook, as a matter of fact, and she didn't know what ball to carry. She did know she couldn't talk about this now with her daughter.

She turned off the ringer on the phone and went to her computer and she booted up and she counted the hours in her head. She'd go till dawn. She'd have fourteen hours, easily. She'd write ten thousand words. Her Windows desktop appeared before her and she loaded WordPerfect and her book came up and Marie Therese, the Southern belle vampire, was standing before the man she loved. He was still whole. He was still human. His blood was still untainted. She wanted him badly. Okay. Josephine's hands went up, her fingers curled, she hung over the keyboard.

And she hung. And hung. Nothing was coming out of her fingertips. And then Josephine noticed that her nail polish was chipped on the forefinger of her right hand. That needed to be fixed. So she went to the master bath and got her nail polish—arterial red—and she threw herself onto the chaise lounge and she tried to patch the chip and that wasn't adequate, not in the least, it all had to be redone, and she took the polish off each fingernail and repainted each one meticulously, and then she did her toes and dried them with a hair dryer, and then she emptied the trash can in the bathroom, and then all the trash cans in the house. In short, she was blocked.

Fourteen hours later the house was freshly clean, every pore on her body had been examined, she'd lingered over a Lean Cuisine dinner somewhere along the way and then over popcorn and then over three glasses of wine, which induced her to take a two-hour nap, which she expected to put all to rights, but it did not.

It was nearing dawn, she figured, and this had never happened on a Mardi Gras night, this silence. Never. She'd been sitting for the past two hours before the computer, punching the Enter key to retain her words whenever the screen saver—a photo of Josephine's house dripping blood from the roof—kicked in. She'd performed every trivial chore she could dream up to keep from writing and she'd kept from thinking about the obvious source of this writer's block, too. But as the grandfather clock downstairs chimed seven, Josephine noticed a thin strip of daylight showing beneath the lowered shade and she cried out in fear, as if she were Marie Therese herself, desperate to escape the sun.

Josephine squared hard around before the words on the screen. Her hands rose. The freshly painted fingertips hovered and hovered and then Josephine pulled back. Her hands fell. She sighed, deeply, wearily. She could write no more for now. And she knew that the LeBlanc House sat in the center of this terrible, wordless night.

* * *

Josephine went out of her house, and before going to Jackson Square, she drove to Magazine Street and parked at the end of a block she'd once known very well. This place had filled her head with voodoo and jasmine in the dark and with the essence of an octaroon girl who was transformed, by the act of her mother, into the undead and who was torn, by her love for a human, between two irreconcilable worlds. Josephine walked along the block, and the coffeehouse and the bookshop and the run of antique stores were closed tight. And there, up ahead, on the other side of the street was the LeBlanc House. When Josephine had first noticed it, Desiree flashed by in an upstairs window instantly, in the arms of the man she loved and could never marry. Now Josephine stood before the house and it was still beautiful and brimming with the stuff of her imagination. It was stuccoed brick washed the color of early afternoon sunlight, and its two-story galleries were lined with wrought-iron swirls of flowers and fruit and vines, and the great shutters at the French windows on the second floor were open. Josephine thought she heard music. She strained to listen, but there was nothing. A dog was barking somewhere. Nothing else. Then even the dog fell silent.

Josephine crossed the street. She hesitated at the realtor sign hung with a red SOLD placard, and then she moved beneath the windmill palms and up the front steps to the door, set off-center to the right of two leaded stained-glass rosette windows as tall as she. Josephine loved this house. Why hadn't she thought to buy it herself? For one thing, to have any house but her father's house never had crossed her mind. And there were a dozen Josephine Claiborne literary sites around New Orleans. Two dozen. She could start buying them and never stop. But standing on the porch of the LeBlanc House, she suddenly felt heavy-limbed with regret. It was true she desperately wanted this place to stay always the same, though she knew that was impossible. Only vampires could live forever. And now she simply felt weary. She thought to turn to go. But something made her step to the door. She cupped her hands around her face and leaned into the glass. A grand staircase led up to the second floor. She put her hand on the doorknob and there was no reason to expect it to turn, but it did. She opened the door and she thought: *they don't even care enough about the place to lock up.* She hesitated a moment and then called, "Hello?"

There was only silence in reply. No one was here. She did not hesitate now. She stepped in.

* * *

And Rafferty stepped forward to the priest. He closed his eyes as the priest's thumb traced the cross of ashes on his forehead—*Remember man that thou art dust and unto dust thou shalt return*—and Rafferty moved away from the altar, up the side aisle. He'd seen Max well ahead of him in the line of penitents and wondered if his son had seen him. He pushed through the doors into the narthex, and there was Max, waiting, a newspaper folded under his arm. As Rafferty approached, Max whipped the paper out and began flipping the pages. "Did you see it?" Max said, though Rafferty was suddenly struck by the cross of dust on his son's forehead. He wanted to reach up and rub it off. "Look," Max said.

Rafferty looked at a full-page ad that screamed STOP THE DESECRATION. Rafferty didn't want to read any more, though he took in the next block of type, only slightly smaller than the first: A PRECIOUS NEW ORLEANS LITERARY LANDMARK IN PERIL.

"I've seen enough," Rafferty said.

"I'll take care of it."

"No, Max." Rafferty tried to keep his voice steady.

Max rolled on. "There's a lot of boilerplate crap about history and literature in there to give it the illusion of rationality, and it's signed 'Fans of Josephine Claiborne,' but the outbursts are actionable and we know who's really behind this."

"Max."

"They know they can't sue, so they try this stunt, turning the public against us. Well, now *we* can sue."

Rafferty reached out and put his hand gently on his son's shoulder. "Max. We should think this through. Ask some basic questions. Is this particular building so important . . ."

"It's important to *me*," Max said, and there was no anger in his voice, no issues of control, only the hurt of a child. "It's for me, Dad." He seemed to hear his own tone. He sharpened his voice and waved the newspaper. "This can hurt us. All over town."

For the second time in two days Rafferty felt panicky, this time at the prospect of his son telling him to choose— Josephine or him. "Let's talk about this later," Rafferty said.

"Don't you trust me?" Max said.

"I do. That's not the issue."

"Then what is?"

"Later."

"You sent me to Harvard . . ."

Rafferty thrashed around for a way to end this for the moment. He said, "Max. Let's argue later. We're standing in a the middle of a goddamn church, for Christ's sake."

Max blinked and then he shrugged and shot his father a little smile. "You're a goddamn good defender of the faith there, Dad," he said, and he turned and went out the doors of the cathedral.

Rafferty stood for a time in the narthex and tried to figure what it all meant. He looked at his watch. Josephine would be arriving any minute. This cleared his head. They'd talk about the LeBlanc House directly. They'd work it through.

So Rafferty stepped out of the cathedral into Jackson Square and he sat down on a bench and he watched the Catholics going in clean and coming out soiled with their own mortality, and a fortune-teller set himself up nearby, ready to resume his alternate view of the future, and a skinny young man took a saxophone out of a case and laid the case open for donations and he started licking his reed. Rafferty looked at his watch. The ashen foreheads drifted by. The musician licked his reed some more, licked on and on until Rafferty wondered if this was his talent, he would lick his reed all afternoon to the delight of a crowd of tourists. Rafferty looked at his watch. She was late.

And it got worse. Rafferty sat, and eventually the saxophonist actually played, and Josephine did not come. Neither did any crowds for the saxophonist, and he stopped and packed his instrument and went away, and the fortune teller fell asleep—didn't he know from his cards that there'd be no customers today?—and Josephine was forty-five minutes late, and then an hour late, and Rafferty rose. He'd been able to suspend all serious thought till he could talk to her but now there was no keeping his worst fears out of his head. She'd stood him up. And the ad was her declaration why.

For a long moment, Rafferty didn't know what to do.

* * *

Along Magazine Street, the restaurants and the coffeehouses and the antique shops and the bookstores were open, the hangovers and the penance of their owners having been dealt with by noon. The LeBlanc House sat implacably beneath its palms and there was no sign of life in the windows. A car whisked by. A bald man trailed behind a small white dog who snuffled past on a leash. Another car ground its gears and accelerated along in the opposite direction, and the street fell silent. The palm fronds quaked almost imperceptibly from a low-grade breeze. And then Rafferty McCue was standing on the sidewalk, contemplating this house.

Max was right. It would make a wonderful restaurant. But Rafferty was paying a very high price. Perhaps higher than he could imagine, even with ashes on his forehead. He sagged before the LeBlanc House, sagged as if he were as old as this place and fallen into shambles. What was the point of coming here? He turned to leave.

But he took a last look at LeBlanc House. It was his, after all. It was Max's. He quaked at this thought as faintly as the palm fronds, and he didn't know why, though he knew it wasn't from pleasure. He stood in suspension for a moment and then he stepped forward, hesitating briefly at the realtor sign hung with the red SOLD placard, and then he moved beneath the windmill palms and up the front steps to the door. He peered in. There was a staircase before him. And for the second time this day a veteran resident of New Orleans who should never have expected a door to be unlocked on an empty house tried the knob.

He instantly followed the swing of the door and he closed it behind him. He stood in the foyer and drew in the smell of the place, deeply, that strange mixture of mildew and old flowers and cooking oil that had burned away years ago and some animal something, which was perhaps just two hundred years of humanity come and gone in this space. He and Max would fill it with the smell of good food and they would fill it with people talking and laughing and taking their ease. Rafferty felt good about what he was doing with his life. And he felt terrible, standing in this foyer, knowing that what he was doing made this woman he'd held in his arms despise him.

He thought to turn around and leave, but the house itself had let him come in. He had to know her. He thought to go to the kitchen. But that felt like a slap in Josephine's face. He should appreciate the place first as she no doubt appreciated it. He looked up the staircase. Max had spoken of the large room on the second floor and Rafferty climbed the stairs.

There was a landing and a turning and he went up and his footfalls grated in the silence and then he emerged into blindness, the light from the French windows wiping his senses clean for a moment in their contrast with the dimness of the stairway and now the great room that lay around him. He stood now facing to the rear of the space, and his eyes adjusted and in the dimness he could see an old trunk and a few tattered boxes against the far wall and a long table listing downward over a missing leg. The floor felt vast. The ceiling was high. There was a vague glimmer of a chandelier in the shadows. He turned to the front of the room and jerked back. Between the two windows lay a body.

Rafferty moved toward it, squinting against the light. It was a woman. She was dead. And then he realized it was her. Josephine, lying on her back on the floor, her hands folded on her chest, her mouth slightly open, her eyes closed forever. He threw himself forward onto his knees, leaning to her, flares of panic streaking through his head, his arms, and he reached out, his hand trembling, and he pulled it back. He couldn't touch her. He had to touch her. This was his fault. And so he bent down, very near, bent to her and he kissed her on her barely parted lips. She was still warm. And she stirred.

He jerked back again. "Thank God," he cried.

Josephine opened her eyes and she looked into the face hovering over her and she thought for a moment that she was in her coffin, that she'd awakened to find the man who would drive a stake through her heart. But no. It was Rafferty. She was merely sleeping. "You should have awakened me," she said.

"I did," he said. "I thought you were dead."

"You think you woke me from the dead?"

"No. I . . . it's OK now. I was wrong."

"Did you kiss me?"

Rafferty was ashamed. He'd taken advantage of her. "I . . . well . . . I thought I was kissing your dead body."

"That's an excuse?" she said, though she knew she wasn't angry. "It's a good thing I woke up. Who knows what else you might've done."

"But if you were dead, you never *would* have known."

"It's hard for me to say, Oh, well, that's OK then. Don't you know how to make up better reasons?"

"Not on Ash Wednesday."

Josephine sat up and leaned back against the wall. "I fell asleep," she said. "I broke into your restaurant and fell asleep. I was up all night."

"Writing."

"Not writing, thanks to you."

"Look," Rafferty said, "I know I'm Catholic, but I can't take all this guilt. I'm still dealing with your ad."

"Ad?"

Rafferty realized at once that Josephine knew nothing about it. He eased himself onto the floor beside her and also leaned against the wall. "It's just something between our kids," he said.

"Our kids." Josephine suddenly felt weary again.

They sat in silence for a long moment. Then Josephine said, "It's a lovely space, isn't it."

"It will be."

"It is now. Has always been." She tapped her forehead with her fingertip. "In here."

Rafferty looked at her and he understood and he smiled. She did not see the smile. She was seeing the floor lit with gas lamps and aswirl with dancers and Desiree and Marcellus spun by, staring deep into each other's eyes. And she heard the music. But it was out of period. Desiree and Marcellus danced to the Masquerade Waltz.

And now Rafferty was standing before Josephine and he was offering his hand and the same music was in his head and he felt the sudden brilliant flare of the chandelier and the music was all around and Josephine took Rafferty's hand and she rose with quite wonderful grace and she slid into his arms and they swirled around the floor onetwothree as if this were the dance they'd danced at the beginning of their story onetwothree and they spun but now the masks were gone their faces were naked and they looked into each other's eyes and they each were ready to say to their children give it up onetwothree and they were ready to touch onetwothree and just as each step they took was as one so too did they stop at the same moment on the same beat and the music played on in their heads onetwothree and Josephine whispered "Bring your face close" and Rafferty did and Josephine rose to him and she bared her teeth and she bit him on the neck, very gently, drawing no blood at all.

* * *

Robert Olen Butler *won the 1993 Pulitzer Prize for Fiction with his collection of stories* A GOOD SCENT FROM A STRANGE MOUNTAIN. *His short stories have appeared in* The New Yorker, Esquire, The Paris Review, Harper's, *and others. He has been honored four times in* BEST AMERICAN SHORT STORIES *and seven times in* NEW STORIES FROM THE SOUTH. *He is the author of two collections of short stories and ten novels. His most recent novel is* FAIR WARNING, *published by Atlantic Monthly Press. He teaches creative writing at Florida State University.*

Sally Shivnan
The Confectioner
from Glimmer Train Stories

————————— • —————————

The old man was bent over with his hands deep in the display case, touching the tops of all the chocolates, noting their smooth, rounded corners, their uniform peaks, his fingers brushing the tickly edges of the paper cups as he moved from the maple creams to the vanilla butter creams, and then to the orange, lemon, and coconut ones. His hands trembled up to the cordial cherries, over the flat pieces of almond bark, alighting on the meltaways. It was a great relief, the bending down, like a rubber band relaxing, though reaching with his arms was a strain. He peered into the sunlit depths of the big glass case. His was a view like looking through crystals of rock candy.

The bells on the door jingled: it was a customer (the teenage boy who worked for him came in, always, through the back door). The old man jerked back from the chocolates and pulled himself upright. He laid his hands on top of the case, avoiding the hazardous shapes there, the gift bags hanging on their little tree, the jar of giant lollipops, and the pyramid of fancy little tin boxes which customers could buy and fill with chocolates.

A woman walked up to the counter, smiling. He knew her; she was after peanut-butter smoothies. She had been coming in for several weeks. She always moved quickly, always in a hurry.

"How are you?" she said.

"Very well," he said, mumbly.

"I'll just have two peanut-butter smoothies."

He obliged her, and took her money. He put the bill in the cash drawer and held out a dime to her. She waited a few moments. The light changed around her as the sun came out from behind a cloud. A truck went by and the window shook.

"I gave you a five-dollar bill," she said, gently.

He nodded and murmured and opened the drawer again, and took out four single bills, and gave these to her without apology. The bills fluttered as they left his hand.

"Thank you," she said, looking at him, staring.

"Very well," he replied, inaudible then as another truck went by.

But after the truck passed, the room was silent. The old man took up his position behind the glass case and stood motionless there. He heard the jingle of the bells again as the door was pulled open. He stooped again as the bells ceased, reaching deep into the case once more to touch where he left off. His fingers found the almond butter crunch, then he patted the chocolate mini-pretzels, lingering on them. But the woman had paused in the doorway, thought to return, closed the door, and was studying him, wide-eyed, as he pawed the chocolates with his trembling hands.

He heard the bells again. He straightened immediately and faced the door. He waited but nothing happened.

"Hello?" he said.

He stood there until his back ached from the strain. The clouds crossed the sun again, changing the light.

"Hello?" he tried again, but then he heard his employee coming in the back door, and forgot his confusion. He remembered, instead, how he needed to talk with the boy, because he was so deeply worried about what was ahead of them, though he doubted the boy had given it much thought.

"Danny," said the man.

"Mr. Feathers," the boy responded.

Danny nodded at his boss and set himself to wiping up the frosting on the table; he'd left it there when he got hungry, knowing he could clean it up when he got back. Stretching over the table made him burp onion from his sandwich. He had offered, as he always did, to bring the old man something back for lunch. He had never seen Mr. Feathers eat anything but a piece of candy, once or twice a day.

Just now Danny looked over and saw him insert a cream into his mouth. The old man turned, facing him, chewing. He saw the boy had stopped work, was standing upright and still; he cleared his throat and said, "Would you like one?"

"No," laughed the boy, and went back to wiping the table. "I tried to bring you lunch," he said. "You never eat nothing."

Danny's arms made wide, smooth arcs over the table's surface. He wore a football shirt, smudged with chocolate, which hung to his bony knees like a dress, hiding the cut-off shorts he wore underneath. His skinny ankles stuck out of basketball shoes that wore a perpetual fine white crust—the sugar grit and flour dust were everywhere, creeping out of corners and coming up from the cracks of the linoleum tile. The steel legs of the table where the boy was working were thinly dusted—even the walls of the place, and the old man's desk and chair, and the old man! Danny wasn't blind to it, but left it be.

Mr. Feathers remembered that he was worried and he shuffled over to his little desk and stood with his nose almost touching the calendar on the wall. He was able to make out the month because he already knew what month it was.

But he was thirsty after eating the chocolate. His tongue stuck when he tried to lick his lips. He began to move to the sink to get a glass of water, a substantial journey because his steps were small.

Danny bumped into him on his way to the sink to rinse his rag, said, sorry, but too softly for his employer to hear. They stood side by side while Danny washed the icing from the rag and stared out the window, whose glass, like everything else, wore a dusting of white, only thick enough to make the world outside a shade paler. He didn't look at the daffodils blooming in the dirt-patch beneath the window, but straight to what interested him more: the back lot of the used-car dealership down the block, where the cars were washed and waxed before they were moved out front. He admired the gleam of red and chrome and glass, shiny even from this distance. Mr. Feathers began waving his arm in the air over the sink.

"What is it? What do you want?" Danny asked, but didn't get an answer. Eventually the old man managed to say, "water," though Danny, by then, was across the floor with a broom, sweeping, and did not hear him. Mr. Feathers continued to reach for a glass whose location he did not know. He touched the faucet but didn't turn it on. He tried to say, "I want a glass of water," but it came out of his throat as just a croak. His arms grew heavy, so that they started sinking in the air as he reached with them. A burning came to his eyes, but he was too dry to make tears. Danny had danced off with his broom to the front of the store—the old man noticed how distant the sweeping sound was.

He gave it up and returned to his desk to sit down. Danny came back and stood looking out the window again, leaning on his broom. At lunchtime, he had walked across the gravel lot he stared at now, had felt light, hungry, had felt the warm sun on his shoulders, the nice openness of space around him. He sighed, turned away from the window. He made a decision.

"I'm going to make the fruit paste," he said. He came over to the sink, took down the big stainless-steel bowl. Mr. Feathers sat quietly in his chair while the boy moved around the room, making noise everywhere, like the sounds of a woman in the kitchen—the ring of a bowl coming to rest on the table, the fall of a spoon in the sink. The old man remembered the photograph on his desk and began to gaze at it in a dreamy way; just like the calendar nearby, he knew the photograph because he already knew it: a picture of his wife and daughter, Judith and Isabel, who had both died a long time ago. Across the room, Danny studied the old man studying the picture. The daughter had died first, then her mother; Danny had no idea when this was, and it hadn't seemed right to ask. In fact, Mr. Feathers wouldn't have been able to answer. With the passage of years, the two losses inched ever closer together in time in his memory, and if pressed he would not have been able to describe his wife and daughter, their hair, their eye color, their ages when they died, the sounds of their voices. "Judith and Isabel," he thought.

The boy rolled out the candy dough on the table. He stretched forward, his shoulders unbinding, loosening, his forearms tensing, his hands tight on the rolling pin. His flat belly pressed the table's edge. Come summer there wouldn't be much to do there. People didn't eat chocolate in the summertime—it melted when the weather got hot—they bought ice cream instead. His friends expected he would quit that job when things got slow.

The old man stirred. He remembered what he was worried about—Valentine's Day was behind them, Easter was coming. He began to speak and Danny had to pause in order to hear him.

"It's time to change the sign," he said.

"We don't have to do that yet," Danny said.

"No, it's time to change the sign."

"I'm in the middle of this, it'll have to wait."

Mr. Feathers thought about the situation. He knew it would take the boy a long time to finish. The sun was moving around to the back window, and the rear of the store, where they were, was warm yellow with the light. Time was slipping away, and he was alarmed—the boy, though, never seemed concerned about important things.

"I'm going to go change the sign," he said. Danny frowned, said nothing. He had a lot to get done that afternoon and only so much time to do it.

The letters for the sign were kept in a plastic bucket underneath the desk. Mr. Feathers picked up the bucket and started for the front door, while Danny continued rolling out the candy. Some moments later the bells hanging on the door jangled stiffly as Mr. Feathers passed out of the building.

He walked the few steps to the sign, and set the bucket down. In his ears the continuous noise of the street carried on—the rising and falling sounds of cars approaching and then fading away, the vans and trucks rushing by. At times, the sounds were complex—brakes and horns, and trucks working to shift up or down. There were two lanes in each direction, and traffic lights both ways. The trucks lifted dust from the road and left the smell of diesel exhaust behind. The old man tasted the street in his mouth.

He began pulling the letters off the sign. His arms were slow but he didn't have to reach high. The bendy plastic rectangles, each printed with a single black letter, came easily out of their grooves; he dropped them in the bucket. The sign rested on wheels, and had an electric arrow which pointed toward the building and which would light up if it was plugged in, but they never plugged it in. It was of the same sort as two other signs farther down the block—the one at the church, whose message changed each week— *God Gives Enough Grace for Whatever We Face*—and the one at the car lot, which never changed—*Used Car Blowout*. A few feet above the electric sign hung another older sign, wooden with tin letters, sticking out over the door of the store. It said *Candy Shopp*, its vestigial *e* long gone.

Once Mr. Feathers had cleared all the words from the sign he stood still a moment, looking at its white emptiness. The bucket beside him was almost full to the top now with letters. He bent down and pulled up a handful, and he held them up one by one to his eyes. He found an *L* and an *O* and dropped the rest back in the bucket, and fitted the two he kept to the top line of the sign. He reached down again, slow, and brought up more letters, his face flushing red now and his breathing huffy as he worked to make out the shape of each one. He found another *O* and an exclamation point he kept as well. His body swayed as a tractor trailer went by, and he dropped the exclamation point on the ground. He would leave it there for now. He stooped again to the bucket: the bend in his knees made his whole frame shake. He managed to lift just one letter. He straightened. The letter was not anything he could use.

The next time he pushed his hands down hard on the letters in the bucket and clamped his fingers around them. He forced his legs straight. He breathed through his mouth, in and out, too fast. Half of his letters fell to the ground. He held onto the remaining ones and stood there, waiting to feel better.

Danny left the table and went to wash his hands at the sink. He shook his head, frowning, picked up the towel to dry his hands, looked out the window, and stared at the gravel. He began to move away, but then stopped, stayed a moment longer, gazing out the window at nothing. He patted his hands with the towel, then balled it up in his fist and threw it down sharply on the counter.

He went out front and saw Mr. Feathers standing there, face to face with the sign, blinking, panting. His fists hung at his sides like weights, each grasping a letter. The sign said *Look Out*, and that was all.

Danny stepped forward. He scratched his head and then stood with his hands on his hips.

"What are you trying to spell?" he asked. He saw all the letters lying around the man's feet. He picked up the bucket. When the old man didn't answer, he said, "What letters do you want?"

Mr. Feathers gasped, "*B*."

Danny flipped through the bucket, found a *B*, began to insert it next to *Look Out*, but Mr. Feathers said, "New line."

He started a second line.

"What is it you're trying to spell?" Danny asked again. He could have worked more quickly if he knew, but the old man wasn't saying. Instead he puffed out the name of each letter with a difficult breath. Together, in this way, they built the words.

"Here," said Danny, "give me those," reaching for the letters the man still held in his fists. He had to lean down and unwrap his fingers from the letters to take them from him. Then he gathered up the ones lying on the ground.

"Come on," he said, and touched the man's elbow.

"No."

"Aren't we finished?"

"Yes."

"Come on then."

"No."

"What do you want?" He stepped back, put down the bucket, stood very still and straight while Mr. Feathers stayed bent over, wobbling. He looked like he might fall over, but the boy did not move to help him. "I have work to do," Danny said, "let's go inside."

"I have work to do," the old man echoed.

"No you don't. You don't have to do nothing. You just have to come in out of the street."

"No." His hands fluttered up to his head as if he was looking for his ears.

Danny grunted and looked around quickly. "I'm going then," he said.

"No!"

The boy stood and stared, with his mouth a little open. "Come on," he begged. "We look silly," he added, softly.

"I'm not silly."

Danny lunged forward, and Mr. Feathers saw the shape coming at him, the tall, strange body coming at him, and it made him fall sideways. His legs were gone, he had no legs, and he thought the boy was going to push him down.

But Danny caught him up in both arms before he quite hit the ground, lifted him, and held him, their two bodies pressed close together, both out of breath. They hung together there, while the trucks and cars rushed by them trying to beat the traffic lights. They were close enough the man could see the boy's thin, smooth face, his eyes and nose, and the boy could see the watery redness inside the old man's lower eyelids, and the way they hung away a little from his eyeballs.

"I'm sorry," Danny whispered, drowned out just then by a passing bus, so that his whisper couldn't be heard.

He kept his arm around Mr. Feathers, steadied his elbows, and began to ease him toward the door. He looked back over his shoulder at their handiwork, as they took their tiny steps together. *Look Out*, it said, *Bunnies Are Coming!*

The bells shook. The boy kicked the door shut with his foot. He continued to guide the old man, through the room, around the counter, to the little desk in the back, left him there and stood in the middle of the sunlit floor, his hands hanging empty, his head turned toward the window. Mr. Feathers could see his form in the haze of light—saw the boy was doing that standing-still thing he did sometimes. He waited for what the boy would do or say next.

Danny examined, briefly, the condition of his fingernails, then looked up at Mr. Feathers. He told him he had a mind to make some of those perfect little Belgian seashells, the ones with the swirls of creamy white in them all curling through the milk chocolate.

* * *

Sally Shivnan's short fiction has appeared in journals including Glimmer Train Stories, So To Speak, *and the* Baltimore Review. *Her travel essays have been featured in* The Washington Post. *She has just completed a novel and is at work on a nonfiction book project, a collection of essays looking at various lost cultures through contemporary eyes. In 1998 she was a Heritage Award recipient, and she recently won a 2002 Very Short Fiction Prize from* Glimmer Train Stories. *She has an MFA from George Mason University and teaches creative writing at University of Maryland, Baltimore County.*

Thomas Sheehan

The Man Who Hid Music

from The New Works Review

———————————— • ————————————

O ne day at the little house where the dowser used to
live a kind-looking man with a beard came carrying
all he owned on an A-frame on his back. He set the A-frame on the ground and looked at the small house needing
much work. Muscles moved under his shirt.

"Whose house is this?" he said to some children playing
at an edge of a field. This was the place where the mountain
came to a rest, but the river had not been found as yet.

One of the boys said, "It used to belong to the dowser,
but he went away." The boy used a stick to walk with as
one leg was slightly crooked and made him lean.

"Why did he go away?" the man said, looking closely at
the stick the boy had to use.

"People laughed at him," answered the boy. When he
looked at his friends some of them began to chuckle and
grin. "Don't," the boy said. His sandy hair caught the wind;
his eyes were hazel and steady.

"If I want to fix this house up and live here, tell me who
I have to see." The children could see some of the tools
hanging on the man's A-frame. On edges where the sun
touched them the tools shone brightly as if they had been
polished with gems.

"See Macklow the mayor. He lives down there where
those walls meet." The boy pointed across the wide fields.
"He'll be on his porch listening to the birds of the fields.
My name is Max. What is your name?"

The man of the tools smiled at Max's description of the

mayor. "My name does not count, only what I do," he said. He walked across the fields and soon had the house to work on. At first it was just the children who watched him fix doors and steps and windows, but soon other people, including Macklow, came to watch. All the time he used tools the man whistled different tunes. At his work he was a happy man.

The house was soon a sparkling and cozy place with no lopsided boards and no broken steps and no windows free to the air. When the man needed wood, he put the empty A-frame across his shoulders and walked off toward the mountain and the forests. In the evening he returned with a pile of wood of all lengths sitting across the back of his shoulders.

"Some day, perhaps soon," he said one day to the children watching him, and a few of the older people, "I will have a surprise for you." As usual, just at dusk, the man took some of his wood he had been working with and brought it inside the little house. The light went on inside so they knew he was still working.

Nobody knew what he was working on. But the light burned long into many nights.

And soon, to everyone's surprise, a garden was also blooming behind the house. Macklow was really surprised because his own fields were slow. Nobody had seen the kindly man walk out of his little house at night, time after time, and put buckets of water on his little garden. The dowser's well was right inside the little house and those who had laughed at the dowser never knew about the well and the sweet water it gave up.

One morning the man came out of his house and gave a new stick to Max. It was much better than Max's old stick, and was smooth and polished and very strong. Max was proud of his new stick and could walk faster with it. Over his head he waved it and showed it off to his friends.

On each morning from then on the man began to build a fence around the house and the garden. At first he put up strong posts, then mounted stringers between the posts. When all the posts and stringers were mounted and connected, he began to place upright pickets on the stringers.

Now and then one of the pickets would cause someone to laugh and titter about its strange shape. Some of the pickets were not as pretty and straight as others. Some indeed looked odd and out of place. But the man kept adding both straight and odd-looking pickets to the fence.

"See," Macklow said one day when village people were talking about the fence, "he brings out what he brought into the house the night before. What he does to it is a mystery, but let us not laugh at him. We laughed at the dowser and he went away in the night. This man is a kind man and has promised us a surprise. Do not laugh at him, no matter what his fence looks like." When he looked at little Max with the new stick, Max and Macklow swapped nods, as if they shared a secret.

But laughter, though, did come each day, at the way the fence looked, at crooked or bent pickets, at the weird shapes of some of them.

Then the day came when all the vegetables in the garden were ripe and the bizarre fence circled the house. The man seemed pleased and put his tools down except for one knife and walked off toward the forest. He came back with one small piece of wood. From that piece of wood he whittled a small whistle. When he blew into the whistle he found only one note, a pure note, but only one note.

There was more small laughter and chuckling, but Macklow, remembering the dowser, thinking about the new ripe garden and his own slow crops, would not laugh. Nor would Max with his new walking stick

One morning the man spoke to some people looking at his crop and studying what he had done to fix the house and the fence he had placed all around it. "I have hidden the music here. Music is a part of the soul. Music is part of the water too. And water is part of the soul. Whoever finds the music I have hidden can have this house, for Macklow says it is mine to give."

Macklow nodded his head.

In the morning the man was gone. The tools were gone. The A-frame was gone.

People pored over the house trying to find the music. They did not know what they were looking for. But they found the dowser's well at the back end of the house and wondered at that. Macklow marveled at the well. However, he made sure none of them disturbed the things the man had done to fix the house.

It was curious. Nobody could find the music. None of them knew what they were looking for. But Max kept playing the whistle and kept hearing the note. He would sit on the porch and blow the whistle until people began to be bothered by it and asked him to stop.

But Max also knew that note deep inside his head.

For weeks people looked for the music. But they did not know what they were looking for.

And then, one morning as he walked past the house, Max hit one of the pickets with his stick.

Oh, how his heart pounded in his chest. How it grew it seemed that it might explode.

It was the same note from the whistle. The exact same, beautiful note.

Back to the gate he went, at the same note-sounding picket and began to walk around the house, his stick slapping against each picket in turn, the way boys have done ever since going by church and school yard fences.

And Macklow looked and the people looked and they all heard the music coming from the fence pickets as Max, walking without his stick support for the first time in his life, played elegant music on the ugly looking pickets with the stick the man had carved. The circled fence played out a whole lovely tune.

And Macklow saw to it that Max and his mother had

themselves a new house to live in at the place where the mountain comes to rest and the river is not yet found.

* * *

Thomas Sheehan *has a Pushcart Prize XXVII nomination from* The Paumanok Review *and nomination for inclusion in* The Zine Yearbook. *His short stories have appeared in the* New Works Review, Electric Acorn, 3AM Publishing, Eastoftheweb, *and* Small Spiral Notebook, *with poetry in* Kota Review, 2River View, Clackamas Review, *and others. His poetry collections include* AH, DEVON UNBOWED, THE SAUGUS BOOK, *and* REFLECTIONS FROM VINEGAR HILL. *He is a co-editor of* A GATHERING OF MEMORIES, SAUGUS 1900–2000, *a nostalgic look at his hometown just north of Boston. His latest novel* VIGILANTES EAST *is available from PublishAmerica.*

Julie Orringer

Note To Sixth-Grade Self

from The Paris Review

———————————— • ————————————

On Wednesdays wear a skirt. A skirt is better for dancing. After school, remember not to take the bus. Go to McDonald's instead. Order the fries. Don't even bother trying to sit with Patricia and Cara. Instead, try to sit with Sasha and Toni Sue. If they won't let you, try to sit with Andrea Shaw. And if Andrea Shaw gets up and throws away the rest of her fries rather than sit with you, sit alone and do not look at anyone. Particularly not the boys. If you do not look at them, they may not notice you sitting alone. And if they don't notice you sitting alone, there is still a chance that one of them will ask you to dance.

At three-thirty stand outside with the others and take the number seven bus uptown. Get off when they all get off. Be sure to do this. Do not stare out the window and lose yourself. You will end up riding out to the edge of town past the rusted gas-storage tanks and you will never find the right bus home. Pay attention. Do not let the strap of your training bra slip out the armhole of your short-sleeved shirt. Do not leave your bag on the bus. As you cross the street, take a look at the public high school. The kids there will be eating long sticks of Roman candy and leaning on the chain link fence. Do they look as if they care who dances with whom, or what steps you'll learn this week? News flash: they do not. Try to understand that there's a world larger than the one you inhabit. If you understand that, you will be far ahead of Patricia and Cara.

For now, though, you live in this world, so go ahead

and follow the others across the street to Miggie's Academy of Dance. There is a low fence outside. Do not climb on it in your skirt. Huddle near the door with the other girls. See if anyone will let you listen. Do not call attention to yourself. Listen as Patricia, with her fascinating stutter, describes what she and Cara bought at the mall. Notice how the other girls lean forward as she works through her troublesome consonants— *G-g-Guess Jeans and an Esp-p-prit sweater*. They will talk the TV shows they watch, who killed whom, who is sleeping with whom; they will compare starlets' hairstyles. None of this talk is of any importance. For God's sake, don't bother watching those TV shows. Keep reading your books.

At four o'clock, go inside with the others. Line up against the wall with the girls. Watch how the boys line up against their wall, popular ones in the middle, awkward ones at the sides. Watch how the girls jockey to stand across from the boys they like. Watch Brittney Wells fumble with the zipper of her nylon Le Sportsac. Don't let her get next to you with that thing. Try to stand across from someone good. Do not let yourself get pushed all the way out to the sides, across from Zachary Booth or Ben Dusseldorf. Watch how Patricia and Cara stand, their hips shot to one side, their arms crossed over their chests. Try shooting your hip a little to one side. Rest your weight on one foot. Draw a circle on the wooden floor with one toe. Do not bite your fingernails. Do not give a loud sniff. Think of the word *nonchalant*. Imagine the eleventh graders, the way they look when they smoke on the bus. Let your eyes close halfway.

When Miss Miggie comes out, do not look at her enormous breasts. Breasts like that will never grow on your scarecrow body. Do not waste your time wanting them. Instead, watch how she moves in her low-cut green dress: chin high, back straight, hips asway. Listen to the way she talks: Fawx Trawt, Tangeaux, Wawtz. Love how she talks, but do not pick it up. When you move North in three years, you cannot afford to say *y'all.* Listen as Miss Miggie describes what y'all will learn that day. Watch how her hand describes the dance steps in the air. Now that the boys are occupied, staring at her breasts, you can look at them openly. Find Eric Cassio. Admire his hair and eyes, but quickly. Like all boys he will feel you looking.

The first dance will always be a cha-cha. On the record they will sing in Spanish, a woman trilling in the background. It will start a thrill in your chest that will make you want to move. Watch Miss Miggie demonstrate the steps. Practice the steps in your little rectangle of floor. Watch how Patricia and Cara do the steps, their eyes steady in front of them, their arms poised as if they were already holding their partners. Now concentrate on dancing. Avoid Sasha and Toni Sue with their clumsy soccer-field legs. Ignore Brittney and that purse. When Miss Miggie looks at you, concentrate hard. Remember practicing with your father. Do not throw in an extra dance step that you are not supposed to know yet. Do not swish your skirt on purpose. Do not look at the boys.

Long before it is time to pick partners, you will feel the tightness in your stomach. Do not let it break your concentration. You have too many things to learn. Remember, if you want to have the most gold stars at the end of the eight weeks, you are going to have to work hard. Imagine dancing in a spotlight at the end-of-class ball, with the best boy dancer from all the seven private schools. On the Achievement Record, next to your name, there are already five stars. Patricia and Cara also have five stars. Everyone else has two or three. Think of the stars in their plastic box. You can almost taste the adhesive on their backs. Two more stars can be yours today, if you do not let yourself get nervous.

When it is time for the boys to pick, do not bite your hangnails. Do not pull at your skirt. Watch how Patricia and Cara lean together and whisper and laugh, as if they don't care whether or not they get picked. Watch how Miss

Miggie brings her arms together, like a parting of the red sea in reverse, to start the picking. The boys will push off with their shoulderblades and make their way across the floor. Do not make eye contact! If you make eye contact you will drown. Do not, whatever you do, look at Eric Cassio. You do not care which one of those other girls he picks. You know it will not be you.

When the picking is over, hold your chin up and wait for Miss Miggie to notice you standing alone. She will take Zachary Booth by the shoulder and steer him over to you. When he is standing in front of you, look down at his white knee socks. Stand silent as he asks, with his lisp, if he can have thith danth. Ignore the snorts and whispers of your classmates. Do not think about Zachary Booth's hand warts. Let him take your right hand and put his left hand stiffly at your waist. Be glad you are dancing with a boy at all, and not with Brittney Wells, as you did last week.

When Miss Miggie starts the music, raise your chin and look Zachary Booth in the eye. Make sure he knows that even though he is the boy, you will be the one to lead. As much as he hates to dance with you, he will be grateful for that. It will be up to you alone to make sure you don't both look like fools. Squeeze his hand when it is time to start. Whisper the steps under your breath. When he falters, keep right on going. Let him fall back in step with you. Out of the corner of your eye, watch Miss Miggie drifting through the room as she claps the rhythm, her red mouth forming the words *one two.* When she looks your way, remember your father's advice: head high, shoulders back. Smile at Zachary Booth. Ignore the grimace he makes in return. If you dance well you may be picked to demonstrate.

And you know which boy will be picked. You know who is picked to demonstrate nearly every time, who Miss Miggie always *wants* to pick, even when she has to pick one of the others just to mix things up. Eric Cassio is not just great in *your* opinion. Already the world understands how excellent he is. The music swells toward its final cha-cha-cha and Miss Miggie's eyes scan the room. Her red lips come together like a bow. She raises her rack of breasts proudly and lifts her finger to point. The finger flies through the air toward Eric Cassio, and Miss Miggie calls his name. He scowls and looks down, pretending to be embarrassed, but there is a smile at the corner of his mouth. Patricia bites a fingernail. Understand that she is nervous. This gives you power. Do not flinch when Zachary Booth pinches your arm; do not let the burning in your eyes become tears. He does not concern you. The only thing that concerns you is who Miss Miggie will point to next. It could be anyone. It could be you. Her finger flies through the air. Is it you? Oh God, it is.

Do not look at Patricia and Cara as they extend their tongues at you. Ignore Zachary Booth's explicit hand gesture. Forget you weigh sixty-nine pounds; stop wanting breasts so badly. So what if you wear glasses? So what if your skirt is not Calvin Klein? For this one moment you have no hangnails, no bony knees; and there is a secret between you and Eric Cassio. When the others clear the floor, look him square in the eye and share that secret. The secret is, you know he likes to dance. It goes back to the day when you were punished together for being tardy, when you had to transplant all the hybrid peas from the small white plastic pots to the big terra cotta ones. Your hands touched, down in the bag of potting soil. When you got cold he gave you his green sweater. Later, as you were cleaning up—the water was running, no one could hear him—he told you he *liked* to dance. Remember these things. The fact that he ignored you at lunch that day, at recess, and every day afterward—even the fact that he is now Patricia's boyfriend—does not matter. He *likes* to dance. Look into his eyes, and he will remember he told you.

Let his arm come around you, tanned and slim. Take his hand: it is free of warts. The dance requires that you maintain eye contact with him almost constantly. Do not be afraid to meet his blue eyes. Smile. Remember what your father has taught you: Cuban motion. It is in the hips. A white boat rocking on waves. The half-hour demonstration with your mother, hair upswept, was not for nothing. Here you are. Miss Miggie lowers the arm onto the record, and the maracas shake into action.

When you dance with Eric Cassio, communicate through your hands. A press here, a sharp squeeze there, and you'll know what he wants you to do, and he'll know what you want him to do. As you change directions, catch Patricia's eye for one moment. Give your hips the Cuban motion. Make her watch. When you twirl, twirl sharp. Listen to Miss Miggie clapping in rhythm. Let all the misery fall out of your chest. Smile at Eric. He will smile back, just with the corner of his mouth. He is remembering transplanting the peas. He does not smile at Patricia that way; that is a smile for you.

Do the special pretzel thing with your arms, that thing Miss Miggie has only shown you once; pull it off without a hitch. End with your back arched and your leg outstretched. Listen to the silence that comes over the room like fog. Remember the way they look at you. No one will applaud. Five seconds later, they will hate you more than ever.

* * *

The next day, watch out. You will pay for that moment with Eric. Wear pants, for God's sake. Take no chances. In gym you will play field hockey; remember that this is not one of your better games. You are on the red team, Patricia and Cara are on the blue. You are left wing forward. When you get the ball, pass it as quickly as you can. What will happen is inevitable, but it will be worse if you make them mad. It will happen at the end of the game, when you are tired and ready for gym to be over. As you race down the side of the field toward the ball, halfback Cara's stick will come out and trip you. You will fall and sprain your wrist. Your glasses will fly off and be broken in two at the nosepiece. You will cut your chin on a rock.

Lie still for a moment in the trampled clover. Try not to cry. The game will continue around you as if you do not exist. Only the gym teacher, leathery-skinned Miss Miller, will notice that anything is wrong. She will pick you up by the arm and limp you over to the bench. Do not expect anyone to ask if you are okay. If they cared whether or not you were okay, this never would have happened. Let this be a lesson to you about them. When Patricia scores a goal they cluster around her, cheering, and click their sticks in the air.

At home, seek medical assistance. Do not let anything heal improperly. You will need that body later. As your mother binds your wrist in an Ace bandage, you will tell her you tripped on a rock. She will look at you askance. Through instinct, she will begin to understand the magnitude of your problem. When she is finished bandaging you, she will let you go to your room and be alone with your books. Read the final chapters of *A Little Princess*. Make an epic picture of a scene from a girls' boarding school in London on three sheets of paper. Push your brother around the living room in a laundry basket. That night, in the bath, replay in your head the final moment of your dance with Eric Cassio. Ignore the fact that he would not look at you that day. Relish the sting of bathwater on your cuts. Tell yourself that the moment with Eric was worth it. Twenty years later, you will still think so.

* * *

That weekend something will happen that will seem like a miracle: Patricia will call you on the phone. She will tell you Cara's sorry for tripping you in gym. Look down at your purple, swollen wrist; touch the taped-together bridge of your glasses. Say it's no big deal. Patricia will ask what you are doing that afternoon. You will whisper, "Nothing." She will ask you to meet her and Cara at Uptown Square.

—We're going shopping for d-d-dresses for the Miggie's b-ball, she'll say. Wanna come?

Now, think. *Think.* Do you really believe Cara could be sorry, that suddenly she and Patricia could crave your company? And even if they did, would you want these girls as friends? Try to remember who you're dealing with, here. Try to tell Patricia you will not go shopping.

Of course, you will not refuse. You will arrange a time and place to meet. Then you will spend half an hour picking out an outfit, red Chinese-print pants and a black shirt, matching shoes and earrings. You will ask your mother to drive you to the mall, and she will consent, surprise and relief plain on her face. She will even give you her credit card.

When you arrive at the entrance to Uptown Square, with its marble arches and potted palms, you will pretend to see Patricia and Cara inside. You will kiss your mother and watch her drive away. Then you will stand beside the potted palms and wait for Patricia and Cara. You will take off your broken glasses and put them in your pocket, and adjust the hem of your shirt. You will wait there for ten minutes, fifteen, twenty. When you run inside to use the bathroom you will hurry your way through, afraid that you're keeping them waiting, but when you go outside again they will still not be there.

You will wonder whether Patricia meant *next* week. You will bite your nails down to the quick, then continue biting.

Stop this. They are not coming.

Go inside. Wander toward the fountain with the alabaster naked ladies. Sit down at the fountain's edge and look at the wavering copper and silver circles beneath the water. Don't waste time thinking about drowning yourself. Don't bother imagining your funeral, with your classmates in black clothes on a treeless stretch of lawn. If you die you will not be there to see it, and your classmates probably won't be either.

Instead, take a nickel from your pocket and make your

own wish: Patricia and Cara strung upside-down from the tree in the schoolyard, naked for all the world to see. Kiss your nickel and toss it in. Feel better. Dry your eyes. Here you are in Uptown Square with your mother's credit card. Go to Maison Blanche, past the children's department, straight to preteens. Tell the glossy-haired woman what kind of dress you want: something short, something with a swirly skirt. Look through all the dresses she brings you; reject the ones with lace and flounces. On your own, look through all the others on the rack. You will almost give up. Then, at the very back, you will find your dress. It is midnight-blue with a velvet spaghetti-strap bodice and a satin skirt. Tell yourself it is the color of Eric Cassio's eyes. Try it on. Watch it fit. Imagine yourself, for a moment, as a teenager, an eleventh-grader, the girls you see in the upper school bathroom brushing their hair upside down and flipping it back. Flip your hair back. Twirl in front of the mirror. The dress costs sixty-eight dollars, with tax. Pay with your mother's credit card. The woman will wrap it in white tissue and seal it with a gold sticker, then slide it into a white store bag. By the time your mother comes to pick you up, you'll have almost forgotten about Patricia and Cara. When she asks you how your afternoon went, lie.

* * *

School this next week will be hell. Everyone will know about Patricia and Cara's trick on you, how you went to the mall and waited. Now you will have to pay a price. People will come up to you all day and ask you to their birthday parties and family picnics and country clubs. Do not dignify them with a response, particularly not crying. This will be extremely difficult, of course. Try to understand what's going on: you got to dance with Eric Cassio and he refused to act as if you made him sick. This is a threat to the social order.

By Tuesday afternoon, things will become unbearable.

It is a dull week—preparations for a Spring pageant, the history of the Louisiana purchase, sentence-diagramming in English—and people have nothing better to talk about. After lunch, on the playground, they gather around you as you try to swing. They needle you with questions: how many hours did you wait? Did you cry? Did you make believe you had a pretend friend? Did you have to call your mommy?

Get out of the swing. Be careful. You are angry. Words do not come easily around these people, particularly when they have been picking at you. But you cannot let them continue to think that they have made you miserable. Tell them you went to Maison Blanche and bought a blue velvet dress.

—Liar! You can't afford a dress.

—I did.

—No, you d-didn't. You wouldn't know how. I think you bought a d-d-d—"

—A *diaper*, Cara finishes.

—It's a blue velvet dress. With spaghetti straps.

—They don't even h-h-h-have a dress like that there. You n-never went in there, you liar. You were too b-busy crying. Waah-aah! No one likes me! You bought a d-d-d-d-dirty baby diaper. You're wearing it right now! Ew, ew.

Ew, ew, ew. They run away from you, holding their noses, and tell their friends you had to wear a diaper because you kept stinking up your pants. Back in the classroom, before the teacher gets back, they push their desks into a tight little knot on the other side of the room. Finally understand the vocabulary word "ostracize." Look away from them. Stare at the blackboard. Swallow. Out of the corner of your eye, glance at Eric Cassio. He will be watching you, not laughing with the others. Patricia will lean over and whisper in his ear, and he will answer her. But he will not—not once—laugh at your expense.

When the teacher comes in and asks what on earth is going on, everyone will start moving the desks back without a word. Soon you will all get lost in the angles and word-shelves of a sentence diagram. After that, math. Then the bus ride home. Now you can spend all evening sulking in the alcove of your bedroom. When your parents come to tell you it's time for dinner, you will tell them you have a headache. You will cry and ask for orange children's aspirin. Half an hour later your little brother will come to you with a plate of food, and he will sit there, serious-eyed, as you eat it.

Later that night you will hear your parents in their bedroom, talking about sending you to a different school. Your father is the champion of this idea. When your mother argues that things might be getting better for you, you will secretly take her side. You tell yourself that leaving the school would mean giving up, letting the others win. You will not have that. You will not go to the schools your father suggests: Newman, your rival, or Lakeside, a religious day school. You will get angry at him for mentioning it. Doesn't he believe you can prove yourself to them, get friends, even become popular?

You blind, proud, stupid, poor dunce.

* * *

Next day, you will bring the dress to school. Why, for God's sake? Why? Won't they see it at the Miggie's Ball anyway? But you insist on proving to them that it's real, despite the obvious danger. You will carry it in the Maison Blanche bag to show you really bought it there. When it's time for morning recess, you casually take the bag out of your locker as if you have to move it to put some books away. Patricia and Cara stop at your locker on their way out. You pretend not to see them. Notice, however, that Eric Cassio is standing in the doorway waiting for them.

—Look, she b-brought a bag of baby d-d-d-d...

—You're stinking up the whole place, Cara says.

You pick up the bag so that the tissue inside crinkles, then steal a glance inside and smile to yourself.

—Is that your K-mart dress for the Miggie's ball?

—Can I b-borrow it? Patricia takes the bag from you and holds it open. You feel a flash of fear, seeing it in her hands. Look at Eric Cassio. He is staring at his shoes. Patricia takes out the tissue-wrapped dress and tears the gold sticker you have kept carefully intact. As she shakes it out and holds it against herself, she and Cara laugh.

—Look at me. I'm Cinderella. I'm Cher.

Tell her to give it back.

—Oh! Sure. C-come and g-get it. Patricia lofts the dress over your head in a blur of blue; Cara catches it.

—Don't you want it, stinky baby? Cara shakes it in your face, then throws it over your head again to Patricia.

Patricia holds the dress over your head. She is three inches taller than you. You jump and catch the hem in one hand and hold on tight. When Patricia pulls, you pull too. Finally she gives a sharp yank. There is a terrible sound, the sound of satin shearing, detaching itself from velvet. Patricia stumbles back with half your dress in her hands. Her mouth hangs open in a perfect O. Outside, kids shriek and laugh at recess. A kickball smacks against the classroom wall.

Cara will be first to recover. She will take the half-dress from Patricia and shrug. Oh well, she says. It was just an ugly dress.

—Yeah, Patricia says, her voice flat and dry. And a stupid b-brand.

She will throw the piece of dress at you. Let it fall at your feet. Suppress the wail of rage inside your ribcage. Do not look at Eric Cassio. Do not move or speak. Wait for them to leave. When the classroom door closes behind them, sit on the floor and stuff the rags of your dress back into the paper bag. Stare at the floor tile, black grains swirling into white. See if you can make it through the next five minutes. The next ten. Eventually, you'll hear the class coming back from recess. Get to your feet and dust off your legs. Sit down at your desk and hold the bag in your lap.

You will remember a story you heard on the news, about a brother and sister in Burma who got caught in a flood. As they watched from a rooftop, the flood stripped their house of its walls, drowned their parents against a bamboo fence, and washed their goats and chickens down the road. Their house is gone. Their family is gone. But they hold onto a piece of wood and kick toward dry land. Think how they must have felt that night, kicking into the flood, the houses all around them in splinters, people and animals dead.

* * *

On Saturday, wear something good. A pair of white shorts and a red halter and sandals. Put your hair in a barrette. Try not to think about the dress in its bag at the bottom of your closet. That does not concern you. Go downstairs and get something to eat. You will not erase yourself by foregoing meals. After breakfast, when your mother asks if you'd like to make cookies, say yes. Look how much this pleases her. You have not felt like doing anything in weeks. Take out the measuring cups and bowls and all the ingredients. Mix the dough. Allow your brother to add the chocolate chips.

Put the cookies in the oven. Check them at three minutes, and at five. Your brother claps his hands and asks again and again if they are ready yet. When they are ready, open the oven door. A wash of sugary heat will hit your face. Pull on the mitts and take out the cookie sheet. Just then, the doorbell will ring.

Listen as your mother gets the door. You will hear her talking to someone outside, low. Then she'll come into the kitchen.

—There's a boy here for you, she says, twisting her hands in her apron. He wants to ride bikes.

—Who?

—I don't know. He's blond.

Do not drop the tray of cookies on the kitchen tile. Do not allow your head to float away from your body. The familiar tightness will gather in your throat. At first you will think it is another joke, that when you go to the door he will not be there.

But then there he is, in the doorway of the kitchen. It is the first time in years someone else your age has stood inside your house. And this is Eric Cassio, in his blue striped Oxford shirt and khaki shorts, his hair wild from the wind. Watch him stare at your brother, who's gotten a handful of cookie dough. Try talking. Offer him a cookie and milk. Your mother will take your brother, silently, out into the yard, and in a few moments you will hear him shrieking as he leaps through the sprinkler.

Now eat a cookie and drink milk with Eric Cassio. Do not let crumbs cling to your red halter. Wipe the line of milk from your upper lip. Watch Eric eat one cookie, then another. When he's finished he will take a rumpled white package from his backpack and push it across the table. You will be extremely skeptical. You will look at the package as if it were a bomb.

—I told my mom what happened at school, he says. She got you this.

Turn the package over. It is a clothing bag. When you open it you will find a dress inside, a different one, dark red with a deep V neckline and two small rosettes at the hip.

—I know it's not the same as the other one, he says.

Look at him, hard, to make sure this is not a joke. His eyes are steady and clear. Stand up and hold the dress up against you. You can see it is just the right size. Bite your lip. Look at Eric Cassio, speechless. Try to smile instead; he will understand.

—Patricia won the Miggie's thing, he says. She told me last night.

For a moment, you feel bludgeoned. You thought it

would be you. You and Eric Cassio. It was supposed to make all the difference. Patricia couldn't possibly have more stars than you. Then remember there's another important thing to ask him.

—Who's the boy?

He looks down into his lap, and you understand that the boy is him. When he raises his eyes, his expression tells you that despite the dress, despite the hybrid peas, things are not going to change at school or at Miss Miggie's. He will not take walks with you at recess or sit next to you at McDonald's. You can see he is apologizing for this, and you can choose to accept or not.

Get to your feet and pull yourself up straight; raise your chin as your mother has shown you to do. Adjust the straps of your sandals, and make sure your halter is tied tight. Then ride bikes with Eric Cassio until dark.

* * *

Julie Orringer is the Marsh McCall Lecturer at Stanford University. She was a Truman Capote Fellow in the Stegner Program at Stanford, and she received her MFA from the Iowa Writers' Workshop. Her stories have appeared in The Yale Review, The Paris Review, Ploughshares, The Pushcart Prize XXV, *and* THE BEST NEW AMERICAN VOICES 2001. *She is completing a short story collection,* HOW TO BREATHE UNDERWATER.

Bill Roorbach
Big Bend
from The Atlantic Monthly

———————————— • ————————————

T hat night Mr. Hunter (the crew all called him Mr.
Hunter) lay quietly awake for two hours before the
line of his thoughts finally made the twitching conversion
to mirage and hallucination that heralded ease and
melting sleep.

What had kept him awake was primarily a worry that
he was being too much the imperious old businessman, the
self he thought he'd conquered—even killed—in retirement,
the part of himself that poor Betty had least admired (though
this was the part that brought home the bacon). This area
of worry he packaged with a resolution only to ask questions
for at least one day of work—no statements or commands
or observations or commentary, no matter what, to Stubby
or anyone else; no matter what, questions only.

Stubby, who was now snortingly asleep in the next bunk
of their nice but spare staff accommodations here at Big
Bend National Park, was not hard to compartmentalize:
Mr. Hunter would simply stop laughing or smiling at or
even acknowledging Stubby's stupid jokes and jibes, would
not rise to bait (politics primarily), would not pretend to
believe Stubby's stories, especially those about his exploits
with women. Scott was Stubby's actual name. He was fifty-
three, an old hippie who had never cut his ponytail or
jettisoned the idea that corporations were ruining the world,
and who called the unlikely women of his tall tales "chicks"
and "chiquitas." Strange bedfellows, Stubby and Mr. Hunter,
who shared a two-bed room in the workers' quarters.

Another cause of sleeplessness was Martha Kolodny of
Chicago, here in blazing, gorgeous, blooming, desolate Big
Bend on an amateur ornithological quest. Stubby called her

"Mothra," which had been funny at first, given Ms. Kolodny's size and thorough, squawking presence, but which was funny no longer, given the startling fact of Mr. Hunter's crush on her, which had arrived unannounced after his long conversation with her just this evening, in the middle of a huge laugh from Ms. Kolodny, a huge and happy, hilarious laugh from the heart of her very handsome heart. The Kolodny compartment in his businesslike brain he closed and latched with a simple instruction to himself: *Do not have crushes, Mr. Hunter.* He was too old for crushes ("sneakers" he'd called them in high school, class of 1944). And Ms. Kolodny was not the proper recipient of a crush in any case. She was under fifty and certainly over 150 pounds, Mr. Hunter's own lifelong adult weight, and married, completely married, two large rings on the proper finger, giant gemstones blazing.

Still other concerns, carefully placed by Mr. Hunter one by one in their nighttime lockers: the house in Atlanta (Arnie would take care of the yard and the gardens, and Miss Feather would clean the many rooms, as always, in his absence); the neglect of his retirement portfolio (Fairchild Ltd. had always needed prodding but had always gotten the job done, spectacularly in the past several years); the coming Texas summer, a summer he might rather miss.

Oh, but Betty, his wife, his girl, his one and only love, his lover, his helpmate, his best friend, mother of their three (thoroughly adult) children, dead of stroke three years. They had planned all they would do when he retired; and when he did retire, she died. So he was mourning not only the loss of her but also the loss of his long-held vision of the future, the thought that one distant day she would bury him. No compartment was large enough to compartmentalize Bitty (as he always called her), but he achieved a kind of soft peace, like sleep, when he thought of her. He no longer experienced the sharp pains and gouged holes everywhere in him and the tears every night. *Count your blessings, Mr. Hunter,* he had thought wryly, and had melted a little at one broad edge of his consciousness, and had soon fallen asleep in the West Texas night.

* * *

The National Park Service hired senior citizens, as part of its policy of not discriminating based on age and so forth, for pleasant jobs at above minimum wage. And because they didn't accept volunteers for the real, honest work that Mr. Hunter had decided to escape into for a salutary year, he signed on for pay, though he certainly didn't need the money. And here in Texas, Mr. Hunter, rich as Croesus and older, found himself shoveling sand up into the back of the smallest dump truck he'd ever seen, half shovelfuls so as not to hurt his back, and no one minded how little he did. He was old in the eyes of his fellows on the work crew—a seventysomething, as Stubby pointed out, working for $6.13 an hour.

The crew was motley, all right: Mr. Hunter, who was assumed to be the widower he was, and assumed to be needy, which of course he was not (in fact, the more he compared himself with his new colleagues, the wealthier he knew himself to be). Dylan Briscoe, painfully polite, adrift after college, who had wanted to go to Yellowstone to follow his ranger girlfriend but had been assigned here the previous summer. He lost his girl, met a new girl, spent the winter in Texas with Juanita from Lajitas, a plainspoken Mexican-American woman of no beauty, hovered near Mr. Hunter on every job, and gave Mr. Hunter his crew name—Mr. Hunter—because Dylan was constitutionally unable to associate the name Dennis with such an old geezer. Freddy was a brainy, obnoxious jock taking a semester off from the University of Alabama. He was leery of Mr. Hunter, disdainful of Stubby, horrible on the subject of women ("gash," he called them collectively), resentful of work, smelling of beer from the start of the day, yet well read and decently educated despite all. Luis Marichal, the crew boss, about whom much was assumed (jail, knife fights, mayhem) but little was actually known, was liked by all, despite his otherness, for saying "Quit complaining" in a scary voice to Freddy more than once. He always had a gentle smile for Mr. Hunter. Finally, Stubby, short and fat and truly good-humored. Nothing needed to be assumed about Stubby, because Stubby told all: he had recently beat a drug habit, was once a roadie for the Rolling Stones, had been married thrice, had a child from each marriage, had worked many tech jobs in the early days of computers, had fallen into drink after the last divorce or before it, and then into cocaine, and then into heroin, had ended up in the hospital for four months in profound depression, had recovered, had "blown out the toxins," had found that work with his hands and back made him sane. And sane he was, he said. This work crew in Texas had made him so.

All of them earned $6.13 an hour, excepting Dylan, hired on some student-intern program with a lower pay scale, too shy to ask for parity, and of course excepting Luis, who'd been crew here many years though he wasn't thirty, and was foreman—Luis made probably nine bucks an hour, with four young kids to support. And in a way excepting Mr. Hunter, who in addition to his $6.13 an hour from the Seniors-in-the-Parks Program was watching his retirement lump sum grow into a mountain in eight figures.

Mr. Hunter shoveled sand with the rest of them, a wash of sand from the last big rain which had made nearly a dune on the shoulder of the road for a hundred yards, a dune dangerous to bicyclists. The crew shoveled into the small dump truck, and Luis drove, if rolling the truck ahead a few feet at a time could be called driving. Mr. Hunter wore comfortable and expensive relaxed-fit jeans. He preferred shoveling to the jobs the other seniors got: cashier at the postcard stand, official greeter, filing associate, inventory specialist, cushy nonsense along those lines.

Mr. Hunter shoveled as lightly as anybody and did not laugh at Stubby's stories and thought of Martha Kolodny for no reason he could make sense of—her laugh from the center of her heart and soul, and her large frame that oughtn't to be alluring to him at all but was indeed, and her braininess. Intelligence always was sexy to him. She was as smart as Bitty and as quick, though Bitty would have called her noisy.

Big Bend here in April after a wet winter was in thorough bloom: prickly pear, cholla, century plants, scores of others, colors picked from the sunset and the sandstone cliffs and the backs of birds. Mr. Hunter, thinking to get some conversation started, asked his first question of the day, knowing the answer in advance: "Dylan, what can you tell us about the subject of love?"

Dylan blushed and said, "Juanita," with evident pride and huge love for his woman. And everyone at once said, "Juanita from Lajitas," which was fun to say and which had become a chant and which they knew Dylan liked to hear. Not even Freddy would say anything that might harm Dylan-boy's spirit.

"You are like me," Luis said. "A steady heart and a solid love."

And Stubby, damn him, said, "Mr. Hunter, what about you?"

"Have you noticed that I'm only asking questions today?" Mr. Hunter replied.

"But I saw you stalking Mothra," Stubby said. "Mothra, Queen of the Bird-watchers' Bus. She's a cute one, she is. Tall drink of water, she is. I'll bet she was one athlete in her day! Iron Woman! Anchor in the freestyle relay! Bench press two hundred pounds, easy. What do you say, Mr. Hunter? You were gabbing with her nearly three hours yesterday in the parking lot there. You were! No, no, sir, you were! You're a better man than I! More power to you! She won't give me the time of day; with you she's laughing and shouting and joking! And she was scratching her nose the whole time, which Keith Richards once told me is the sure sign you're going to get a little wiggle in."

All work (such as it was) ceased. Mr. Hunter made a game smile and smiled some more and enjoyed the breeze and the attention. He asked a question: "Do you know that Plato's *Republic* begins with a discussion of just this subject—of love and sex? And do you know that one of the fellows sitting around Socrates says something like 'I saw Sophocles'—the old poet, he calls him—'I saw the old poet down in town the other day, three score and ten, and I asked him: At your age, Sophocles, what of love?' And do you know what Sophocles told that man? Sophocles told that man, 'I feel I have been released by a mad and furious beast!'"

The crew stood with eyebrows raised a long time, absorbing this tale from the mysterious void of time that was Mr. Hunter's life.

After a long silence Stubby said, "Oh, fuck you."

Mr. Hunter knew what Stubby meant: the implied analogy was faulty. And Stubby was right. Martha Kolodny was certainly on Mr. Hunter's mind, Martha Kolodny of all women, and the mad and furious beast had hold of Mr. Hunter certainly. It wasn't as if he'd had no erections in the past three affectionless years—but the one he'd had this morning caught his attention surely. And it wasn't all about erections, either. It was that laugh from the heart and the bright conversation and something more: Martha Kolodny could *see* Mr. Hunter, and he hadn't been seen clearly in three years. Nor had his particular brand of jokes been laughed at, or his ideas praised, nor had someone noticed his hair (still full and shiny, and bone-in-the-desert white) or looked at his hands so, or gazed into his eyes.

* * *

At the Thursday-evening ranger's program a very bright young scientist lectured about Mexican fruit bats with passion, somewhat mollifying Dennis Hunter's disappointment. Oh, in the growing night the assembled travelers and rangers and tourists and campers and workers (including Stubby) did see bats, as promised. And among the assembled listeners were a number of birders from Martha Kolodny's bus. But Martha was not among them.

Dennis Hunter lurked on a back bench in clean clothes— Hong Kong-tailored white shirt, khaki pants, Birkenstocks (ah, retirement), eight-needle silken socks—trying to remember how long Martha had said her birding group would be here. Until April 17 was the date he remembered, almost his second daughter's birthday; his second daughter was, yes, about Martha's age. Five more days, only five.

Then he felt a sweeping presence and heard a suppressed laugh from deep inside the heart of someone's capacious heart, and Martha stood just beside him. "May I sit?" she asked. This was a whisper, but still louder in Dennis's ear than the ranger's lecture. She sat on his bench and slid to his side like an old friend; got herself settled, deep and quiet, her perfume expansile; put her chin in the air and raised her eyebrows, seeming to try to find her place in the stream of words as the passionate ranger introduced a film.

The heavy narration covered the same ground the lecture had, with less fervor and erudition, but the pictures of bats were pleasing to watch: the film employed all sorts of camera and lighting tricks and slow-motion tricks and freeze-frames and animation. Bats streaming out of Carlsbad Caverns, not eight hours from here. "Always wanted to see that," Martha said, leaning into Dennis. "Always, always."

"I thought for you it was birds," Dennis said.

Martha put a hand to her nose and scratched. "Whatever has wings," she said. Her other hand was on the bench close between them, and she leaned on it so that her head was not a breath away from Dennis's. He smelled her shampoo—coconut and vanilla. Her henna-red hair, braided in a thick lariat, her distinct chin, the strong slope of her nose, her deep tan, her wrinkles from laughing from the heart of her, her wide shoulders and loose white shirt—all of it, all of her, was in his peripheral vision as he watched the film, which was more truly peripheral though he stared at it, her many scents in his nostrils.

The night before, they had taken care of the small talk and more: Martha Kolodny was an arts administrator, which title Dennis pretended not to understand, though he knew well enough what it meant. She was the kind of person he had disdained in his years as a marketing wizard at Pfizer (years he had then told her about). Talking to Martha, he'd felt the truth of something Bitty had once said: he had really grown up after sixty-five. Martha had patiently explained that she ran a grants-writing office that helped to provide funding (not such huge figures as Martha seemed to think) for several arts organizations, the Lyric Opera of Chicago among them. She herself had once danced—modern dance— with high hopes. She was too *big*, she had said daintily. "My teachers always said I was too *big*." And she had laughed that laugh that came from the heart of her heart and smote Dennis.

Her husband was a medical scientist at Northwestern, both a Ph.D. and an M.D. His first name was Wences. He was first-generation Polish. He was working on neuro-receptors, about which Dennis knew a thing or two from his years with the drug company. The couple had no kids; they had married late and had decided that at her age kids were not a good idea. Now she was forty-seven. Wences and she barely saw each other. For them the passion had fled. "I'm caught," she had said. "I'm caught in an *economic arrangement*." Her eyes had been significant, Dennis thought.

The film ended abruptly. The ranger-scientist took the podium in the dark that followed. A spotlight hit his face. Martha sat up and looked at Mr. Hunter fondly; that was the only word for how she looked at him—like an old friend. She whispered, "One Batman joke from this boy and we're out of here!"

In a television voice the ranger said, "That's the Bat Signal, Robin."

"That's it," Martha said, feigning great shock. She rose

and took Dennis's hand and pulled him ungently to his feet, and the two of them left the natural amphitheater and were soon striding along a rough path that led into the Chisos Mountains night.

"I knew you'd be at the talk!" Martha said.

"I'm not there now," Dennis said.

She said, "I can't get you out of my head!" She was breathless from the walk. They pulled up at the farthest end of a loop path that looked out over the great basin of the Rio Grande under brilliant, coruscating stars.

"I shoveled sand all day with the boys. Thinking of you."

"I love when you grin just like that," Martha said hotly.

But you are married, Dennis thought to say. He held the words back forcibly. What if she didn't mean anything romantic at all? What an awful gaffe that would be!

They looked out into the blackness of the valley and up into the depths of space and were quiet a long ten minutes. "Mexico over there," Dennis said.

"You know you can rent a canoe and paddle across the Rio Grande to Mexico for lunch? No customs inspection necessary."

He said, "Someone did say that. And at the hot springs, apparently, you can swim across pretty easily. But no lunch."

"Unless you brought your own," Martha said.

"And the hot springs are very nice, too, I hear. Nice to soak in, even in the heat, I hear." He'd heard all this from Freddy in the grossest terms. Freddy had said it was the place he'd bring a *bitch,* if there were anything but *stanking* javelinas around here.

"I would like to kiss you," Dennis said. He'd forgotten entirely how this sort of thing was done, knowing only that now (this he'd read), here in the twenty-first century, one got permission for everything, each step, before proceeding.

"I told my husband I wouldn't mess around with anyone while I was in Texas," Martha said. Then, less lightly, "That's the shambles our marriage is in."

"Well, Martha, darling, a kiss is certainly not necessary to a good friendship," Dennis said, glad he'd asked and not just invited rebuff and embarrassment, though he was embarrassed enough.

But Martha kissed him, full on the lips, and he was glad for the Listerine he had swilled and glad that life hadn't ended and glad to remember all the electrical connections and brightened cells and glowing nerves he was remembering from the bottom of his feet to the tip of his tongue as he kissed her and was kissed.

They talked and necked—no better expression for it—for an hour under the stars.

"Well," Dennis said, "I'm afraid, despite best intentions, you have kissed in Texas." He felt bad for Wences Kolodny.

"But I have not messed around," Martha said.

"On technicalities are the great cases won."

She said, "Do you want to take a little swim to Mexico tomorrow?"

"I'll unpack my swimming trunks."

"I said nothing to Wences about messing around in Mexico."

"That isn't funny to me," Dennis said.

But they kissed till near eleven, when the Chicago birders' bus loaded quickly and headed to the birders' hotel, on the outskirts of the enormous national park.

Dennis walked back to his room with feelings he hadn't had in fifty years, pain both physical and metaphysical, elation sublime. Ambivalence scratched and snarled like an enraged animal under his squeaky cot.

* * *

Mr. Hunter no longer had the physical strength of his estimable colleagues on the work detail, but they had not his old man's stamina. With his steady work all day he outperformed the college boys, though Stubby could do in a single hour more than the whole crew did in all of a typical day when he got inspired, which he did just before lunch on this day, Friday. Stubby worked like a dog and a demon and an ox, worked as if possessed—every cliché applied. He said, "We don't want Luis in trouble if this sand ain't up and off the road, boys!" They'd got about a quarter of it up the previous day, and already, by noon this day, two quarters more.

The crew stopped for lunch and ate in tired silence. Then, as they settled down into what should normally have been something like a siesta, Stubby turned to Mr. Hunter. He said, "Where did you and the bird lady go last night when you left the lecture so early?"

"Why do you ask?" Mr. Hunter said wryly, as the attention of the crew fell pleasingly upon him.

"I was only worried, is all," Stubby said, even more wryly.

After a long silence Luis grinned and said, "Tell us, Sophocles, old poet, what of love?"

"Love!" Stubby said. "You should have smelled our room in the night! What perfume! And perfume, my brothers, does not rub off without some rubbing!"

Still wryly—he could think of no other safe tack to take—Mr. Hunter said, "Do you imply that an old man should not seek romance?"

"Not s'long as it's with an old lady," Freddy said.

"She's not as old as all that," Stubby said. "She's not yet my age, and I'm a youth, as you can see."

"Is she over forty?" Dylan asked helpfully. Embarrassed, he bit into his burrito and looked out over the dry valley of the Rio Grande.

"Ah, forty!" Stubby said. "Forty is the youth of old age and the old age of youth!"

Freddy said equably, "How old are y'all, anyway, Mr. Hunter?" He leaned a long way, gave a short smile, reached and took one of Luis's tortillas.

"Three score and fourteen," Mr. Hunter replied. "Seventy-four. The youth of death, I would say, if pressed."

"What of love, Sophocles?" Luis said again.

Mr. Hunter could not help himself. He beamed. He said, "Do any of you really believe my private hours are any of your business?"

Stubby said, "Do we not have the right to learn from those older than us? And do you, Mr. Hunter, not have the duty to teach us?"

"Tay-ake her to Viagra Falls," Freddy said.

"Mr. Hunter has twice the cactus you have, hombre," Luis said.

"It's not all about sex," Dylan said.

"Hey, I don't know," Stubby said. "This woman, this bird-watcher, Mothra, obviously she's looking for something her marriage isn't giving her. She's taking power here. She's taking care of her needs. She's unfulfilled."

Dylan said, "But she made a promise."

"What is the nature of the promise we make in marriage?" Mr. Hunter said. He tried to sound wry, playing Socrates, but this was too close to the heart of his worry.

Dylan said, "That we should love, honor, and obey."

"The flesh is weak," Luis said opprobriously.

"The flesh has a job to do," Stubby said.

"I say go for it," Freddy said.

A long silence followed in the windless day, punctuated erratically by the squawks of Mexican jays.

"I don't see how," Mr. Hunter said.

Freddy said, "Well, the boy kisses the girl ..."

And the crew laughed, except for Luis. He said, "And what of your wife in heaven? What will happen when you see her there?"

Only Mr. Hunter had seen Luis as religious before now. The air grew more serious. Everyone stared off, each in his own thoughts.

Then Stubby said, "Actually, there's probably more here than the moral question. You've really fallen for this chick, you know? How are you going to feel if it goes further and then—boom—she's back to her husband? Leaves you alone! That's going to be a blow!"

"When Tina broke up with me ... " Freddy said. The others waited, but that was all he managed. Freddy looked off into the sky, and for the first time they could see his heart in his face and think of him as tender.

"There might be that kind of price," Stubby said.

"This is good advice," Mr. Hunter said. "I don't know if I could tolerate the aftermath of a one-night stand."

Stubby slid off his rock, leaned back against it, and closed his eyes. Dylan lay down, chewing a twig. Luis stood, stretched, patted Mr. Hunter's shoulder, and walked up the road to be alone. Luis prayed after lunch, Mr. Hunter knew. He might have thought Freddy was softly weeping if he didn't know what a tough customer Freddy was.

Mr. Hunter had made up his mind: no married woman for him.

* * *

Stubby had joked that Martha was an athlete, and so she was: forty-seven years old, Dennis Hunter's height and weight, she walked with the physical confidence of an athlete, looking in her shorts and stretch top as if she might jump up and fly at any moment. But in Dennis's little rental car her folded legs seemed delicate and soft. Her skin was beautiful to him, and her smell, and her voice.

"I couldn't sleep all last night," she said.

"I could barely work today," he said.

The rest of the talk on the hour's drive to the Hot Springs canyon was about the landscape of the park, and they didn't need to say much for looking at that landscape, the great buttes and cliffs and mesas miles away and unmoving. Martha read from her guidebook: "The park is eight hundred and one thousand one hundred sixty-three acres."

Dennis Hunter hadn't known that.

She read, "The Rio Grande was known to the Spanish

conquistadors as the Great River of the North, and to the early pioneers as the River of Ghosts."

"I'm told this was Comanche territory," Dennis said. Luis had told him so.

Martha nodded her head, shook it, and then nodded it. "Comanche territory," she repeated, saying it from the heart of her heart, where her laughter came from.

Oh, God. Dennis felt his heart flowing out to her entirely, yet not leaving his rib cage at all. They drove slowly through the great basin of the River of Ghosts, past the Chisos Mountains. A pickup truck with New Mexico plates zoomed up from behind, passed easily, zoomed out of sight. Dennis thought about how easily he could declare his love and ask dear Martha her intentions. Perhaps Wences was out. Perhaps a split was imminent. How ask? He said, "'Chisos' means something like 'ghostly' in the Apache language." Luis had told him that, too.

They were just quietly driving along, looking at the landscape. "Yes, it is," Martha said. "Ghostly, all right." She put her hands up in a gesture of amazement. She had taken off her rings. "Living things don't belong here. Not people, certainly."

Dennis felt himself and the car almost lifting off the pavement. Not that he was faint—not at all. If anything, he felt more present, floating car and all, with warm blood in his air-conditioned face and something humming in him, thighs to lungs. She'd taken off her rings. Dennis had never taken his ring off, not once for any reason, not since the night it went on his finger, June 11, 1947.

In the small canyon where the hot springs lay, they walked in the bright sun along seabed cliffs, striated layers of the ages thrown up by earth forces at odd angles. Martha immediately heard a great horned owl, and got it calling to her by hooting saucily. Dennis floated; he floated along the dry path and felt that Martha floated too.

Together they inspected the abandoned ruins of the old hotel and store there, the hotel and store about which

Martha had read aloud from her guidebook. Together they found the petroglyphs she had read about, and walked along a Comanche path that had become a commercial enterprise's trail to the hot springs and was now a park path for tourists. Martha took Dennis's hand. He wanted to declare his love. How old-fashioned he knew he was! She would laugh at him, he thought, and this laugh would come from her teeth and not her heart.

The path descended between thick reeds and willows and the canyon wall. Soon Martha stopped and put a finger in the air. "Hear the river?"

Yes, Dennis heard it, a rushing sound ahead. Martha's hand was in his, their dry hands casually clasped, pressure of fingers in a small rhythm, a pulse of recognition: something profound between them.

Dennis couldn't find the words as the Rio Grande came into view: "Doesn't it ... isn't it ... doesn't this just ... *tickle* you?" That was pathetic. He thought and tried again: "This little sprite of a muddy river, this ancient flow, this reed-bound oasis? That this is the famous border?"

"Dennis, I don't know what to do."

"That that is Mexico over there?"

"May I see you in Atlanta?"

They stopped on the plain and dusty rock—flat, polished sandstone, solidified mud. They stopped and held hands and looked at the river and could not look at each other.

She said, "What is this between us?"

Dennis could think of words for what was between them. It was passion, nothing less, on the one hand, and her husband, nothing less, on the other, both between them and no way to say a word at this moment about either. He let a long squeeze of her hand say what it could, and then he pulled her along. Brightly he said, "I expected gun turrets and chain-link fence and border stations."

"Well, there's nothing but desert for hundreds of miles. They just don't watch much here."

Pleasingly, no other soul occupied the hot springs, a

steady gush of very hot water rising up out of a deteriorated square culvert built a century past. The buildings were gone—swept away by floods, they must have been. But one foundation remained, and formed a sort of enormous bathtub the size of a patio. In the hot air of the day the water didn't steam at all. Soft moss grew in the tub.

Martha sat on a rock and took her shoes off. Dennis liked her feet. He wondered if Wences liked her feet. He liked her knees very much. He liked that she was so strong and big, so unlike Bitty, who was a bone. He liked the fatty dimpling of Martha's thighs in her black shorts. She dipped her feet in. "Wow, hot," she said.

"Maybe too hot for today?" Dennis said.

"No, no, it's wonderful! And then the river will feel cold. A blessing." Then she said, "Well, no one's around." And she pulled off her shirt, just like that, and clicked something between her breasts to make her bra come loose, and shed it, and stepped out of her shorts and then her lacy panties (worn for him, he was startled to realize) and slipped into the hot water in a fluid motion, Dennis more or less looking away, looking more or less upward at the cliff (cliff swallows up there).

"I'm not sitting here alone," Martha said.

So Dennis tried a fluid kind of stripping like hers, but ended up hopping on one foot, trying to get his pants past his ankles. He stripped, and hopped, and slid into the hot water, self-conscious about his old body, the way his skin had become loose, the spots of him.

"It's love between us," he said, which was not the same as declaring love. "And that you are married."

"No touching in Texas," Martha said, far too lightly.

The water was shallow. She sat bare-breasted, up to her waist in the hot water, not exactly young herself. The water was gentle and very hot and melted them both, turned them red like lobsters.

"Swim," Martha said. She climbed out of the pool, down old steps into the river, and dropped herself into the current.

Stroke, stroke, out of the current and she was standing on the bottom again, waist-deep. She was forty-seven, and married, and standing waist-deep and naked in the Rio Grande River, not twenty feet from Mexico. Dennis felt her gaze, considered Wences, heard Luis's stern voice, heard Freddy's (*go for it*), heard Bitty's funny laugh, thought of his three children, heard his daughter Candy (*Daddy, I know Mother would want you to date*), and followed Martha into the river, enjoying the relative cold of it after the scalding spring. Stroke, stroke, stroke, he was being swept away in the current; he pictured himself washed up on a flat rock dead and naked miles downstream. But Martha got hold of his hand, laughing, and they stood waist-deep together in the stream rushing past, silty, sweetly warm water.

"I'll get our stuff," Martha said.

She swam back and bundled everything—large towels, clothes, binoculars, bottle of wine—and easily swam with one arm in the air till she was back by Dennis's side, holding the bundle all in front of her chest, dry. And if not absolutely dry, what difference? It would dry in seconds in the sun and parched air.

Suddenly she said, "The American Association of Arts Administrators conference is in Atlanta this year." They stood in the flow of the river. "I could stay a week with you," she said. "Maybe more. It's June. Only two months from now."

"After that?" Dennis said.

Solemnly she said, "We shall see what we shall see." Then she laughed from the heart of the heart of her, and Dennis laughed and stumbled, and they made their way through the water to Mexico.

"I hope no one shoots us going back," Dennis said.

They made the rocky shore in Mexico and walked, not far, walked in Mexico until they were out of sight of the hot springs across the river, and right there under the late sun she spread the blanket and right there hugged him naked and the two older Americans in Mexico kissed and Dennis

Hunter was a young man again—no, really—a boy in love, a tanned and buff shoveler of sand, a repairer of trails, a knower of animals, a listener to birds, anything but a widower alone in Atlanta the rest of his miserable days, miserable days alone.

* * *

Bill Roorbach, *a 2002 NEA Fellow, is the author of five books, including the Flannery O'Connor Award winning collection of short stories,* BIG BEND. *Other books are:* THE SMALLEST COLOR, *a novel;* INTO WOODS, *essays;* SUMMERS WITH JULIET, *a memoir; and* WRITING LIFE STORIES: How to Make Memories into Memoirs, Ideas Into Essays and Life Into Literature. *Bill is also the editor of the Oxford anthology* CONTEMPORARY CREATIVE NONFICTION: THE ART OF TRUTH. *All are in print, with a seventh book,* TEMPLE STREAM, *forthcoming from Random House / Dial Press.*

Patry Francis

Limbe

from The Antioch Review

———————————— • ————————————

He was maybe four years old, with one of those oversized prophet names some people like to give their babies. Ezekiel. Zebediah. Something like that. But I just called him Limbe. People said they hadn't heard him talk in over two years, but he spoke up in a clear voice that first morning I found him standing outside my door. Within a week, he had returned five times, always with the same request. "Limbe?" he said, asking for one of the frozen ices my Puerto Rican neighbor sells to the neighborhood kids for fifteen cents apiece. Most of them are nothing but frozen Kool-Aid in a cup. But the more popular ones are the exotic flavors like tamarindo or coco. For some people, it's a taste of home; for others, it's a poor man's trip to the islands. Mrs. Bonilla charges a quarter for the kind she makes with real coconut. All the other kids in the neighborhood seemed to find their way to the right door just fine, but not Limbe. And when I complained to his mother about it, she just stood there apologizing all over herself. She had told the boy to count four doors from their apartment and then knock, she said. But since Limbe couldn't count past three, he always ended up at my place.

The mother's name was Cinda and she had a real husband who left the house every day for a real job. That put her ahead of most of the women here; the fact that she kept her kid in clothes that looked like they'd been pressed with a real iron put her another few paces ahead. But you wouldn't know it to look at her. She had this scared way of moving through her life that made me want to slap her on a bad day. On a good day, I just wanted to cover her mouth before she had time to say how sorry she was for taking up space on the sidewalk, for cluttering up my line of vision, for sucking up oxygen that could have been put to better use.

One day I asked Junie about her. People say Junie's a strange friend for an old lady like me. Nineteen years old, and going to art school on a scholarship, he lives down the hill with his grandmother and a couple cousins. But the truth is, Junie's the only one I really talk to here. For one thing, he knows everything that happens in the Heights. It's not that he's nosy or anything. It's just that walking around with a sketch pad all day, he learns things. He says it's not getting in people's business; it's just *looking*, really seeing the person in front of you.

And Junie says there's a reason for Cinda's sorry ways. He says the real live husband who goes to work every day yells so much the police had to come and shut him up a few times. Once Junie got up the nerve to ask if he could sketch her. "You want to draw *me*?" Cinda said, touching her face like she forgot she had one. For a minute, Junie said, she looked flattered, but then she sank back into her scared self. "I don't think my husband—" she began, but never finished. "Sorry . . . ."

Anyway, it didn't matter what I thought of the mother who forgot she had a face or the father who left the apartment every day in a necktie and an old pair of shoes that had been polished to death. It didn't matter what I thought of his crummy job at some department store that didn't even pay enough to get the family out of the Heights, and sent him home screaming so loud it took a cruiser to shut him up. No, none of that mattered. What mattered was the child, the child who was finding his way to my door with increasing regularity.

I was lying in a tub soaking the smell of old out of my skin the first time I heard the knock. A knock obviously made by a child's fist, so light it might have been a bird pecking at a tree. Figuring whoever it was would soon disappear, I didn't move. But later when I was at my vanity painting myself a new face, I heard it again: *peck, peck, peck*. Since I was late for a funeral, I continued to ignore the pesky sound. But it seemed that boy had what my mother used to call biblical patience. What he wanted didn't have to happen any time soon—not today, or this year—not even in his generation. Soon as you looked in his eyes you knew it: this child had *time*.

When ignoring him didn't work, I hauled out my scare tactics. "No limbe here!" I said, leaning so close to his face that I could smell the baby on him. That soap his mama used on his hair. Even before I began to shrink up, I barely reached five feet tall. Still, I learned long ago that being scary isn't about size. Even the junkies know better than to mess with me. Junie doesn't believe me when I tell him how I chase the drug crews away with my eyes. He says no one's scared of an old lady like me; I just got nothing worth their time. But I know different.

Not that I was always this way. In fact, I used to be a little bit like Limbe's mother when I was young, back when I had everything to lose, a husband in the kitchen polishing his shoes, and five babies who smelled so good you stood still and took a deep breath every time one of them walked in the room. But after the fire that left nothing behind, not even a photograph, I gave up fearing things: sickness and death, and people walking around with knives and guns and habits that made them crazy. After the night when I got home from work just in time to see my house turning to ash, the only thing that has scared me has been the sound of my own breath, the weedy way I cling to this earth. *Burned to the ground*, that was how they described the house where I lived Cinda's life. But what they don't know is that the blaze never went out. You don't believe me, just look in my eyes. If anything, that fire only burns hotter the longer I live.

But even the flame behind my eyes didn't scare little Limbe. He wanted what he wanted: something so sweet and cold it burned his hands, something sticky that dribbled down his chin, and onto his shirt, covering his mother's clean ways, the string of apologies she tried to wrap him up in. He stared up at me with two fingers jammed in his mouth, his eyes full of that want. By then, he had given up naming the treat he was after; we both knew. For a long moment, I stood there hugging my robe, half made up for my funeral, one eyebrow painted into a sharp black line, the other one skimpy and naked. I raised the painted eyebrow, making it twitch, thinking that might scare the boy away, but Limbe only laughed. He laughed until the two fingers dropped out of his mouth, revealing a perfect row of baby teeth; and I couldn't help laughing with him.

The next day there were no good funerals in the paper so I gave in. I got me some grape Kool-Aid and a pack of Dixie cups, and made up my first batch of limbe. But for the next week, the boy didn't show. As the heat escalated, I took to sucking the ices myself. They were too sweet— not nearly as good as Mrs. Bonilla's coco limbe; but whenever I ate one, I thought of the boy. I thought of the way he stood on my front stoop laughing, and how the inside of his mouth had been like pink velvet. Whenever I went outside, I looked for him. He wasn't in the playground, nor was he riding his big plastic trike around the sidewalk.

One afternoon when I spotted Cinda heading into the laundry room with a basket of clothes, I pulled a few clean towels out of the linen closet, tossed them in my plastic basket, and followed her. As soon as she heard someone opening the laundry room door, Cinda lowered her head so she wouldn't have to talk. *What's wrong with you?* I wanted to say. But instead, I just started singing real loud. The girl looked so down I was hoping to lift her up with my song, but what came out was a depressing old Billie Holiday number, "Strange Fruit." I don't know what got me started on that song, but it came belting out like it had a life of its own. Cinda just stood there gaping, temporarily forgetting she wasn't supposed to be here. "Wow, you're good, Mrs. Jenkins," she said. "You ever sing professional or anything?"

"Oh sure, I sang with all the greats. Duke, Dizzy, all of them. Bird was my favorite though. You ever hear of Bird?" I knew she hadn't; none of the people her age listened to the old stuff anymore. And it was one of my personal missions to make them feel a little bit guilty about it.

"Bird? Yeah, I think I heard some of his stuff before," Cinda said, a hint of apology creeping into her voice. For once I almost regretted trying to educate the young about their history.

"That's okay," I said. "I don't know much about your music either. What you listen to? Those people who talk-sing?"

By then Cinda had turned back to the safety of her laundry. Whites she was washing that day. Mostly her husband's frayed-around-the-collar shirts for work. "I don't listen to music much," she said.

"That don't surprise me," I muttered. When I saw her throwing in one of Limbe's little T-shirts, I said, "I haven't seen your boy around."

"Isaiah's hasn't been out much; he's had the chicken pox," Cinda said. "I hope he hasn't been bothering you . . . ." She sounded like she knew how often I've thought of belting her one.

"I just told you I haven't seen the boy, didn't I?" I said, pulling the towels that weren't even dirty in the first place out of the washing machine. I know the girl must've thought I was crazy, but it was one of my slapping days, and I wasn't about to stand there and listen to another one of her fool apologies.

On the way out of the laundry room, I slammed the door so hard that I could almost feel Cinda quaking inside. Then I went back to my apartment and made up another batch of grape limbe. When I was done, I took an ice from my first effort and went out on my front stoop. Several times I looked toward the apartment the boy shared with his sorry mother and his screaming father. I half hoped I'd see him come out his door, and laugh at me the way he had the last time I saw him. But it was a few more days before the boy appeared. He looked thinner, and there were chicken pox scars on his face. But his voice, the want in his eyes was as strong as ever. "Limbe?"

When I came back with a grape limbe, he smiled so wide I got another glimpse of that pink velvet. He pressed two coins into my hand. After he had disappeared down the sidewalk licking the top of his limba with satisfaction, I stood there for a moment, wondering what to do with the fifteen cents. Then I went in the house and got an old jelly jar, which I labeled with masking tape. Limbe. But I wasn't thinking of the treat; I was thinking of the boy.

Before the month was up, my jar was nearly full and I had made limbe in every flavor that Kool-Aid ever invented. My own personal favorite was Passion Fruit. By the time I had worked up to the exotic flavors, Limbe had taken to eating his treat on my stoop. Since he never talked, I occasionally joined him. There on some of the most perfect summer days God ever created, Limbe and I sucked our ices in the kind of comfortable silence you can only share with someone who knows you to the bone.

One day the boy appeared with a quarter instead of the usual fifteen cents. "Limbe," he said. "Coco limbe."

"What—do I look Spanish to you?" I said. "I don't know how to make no coco limbe."

I returned with two of the cherry ones I had made earlier in the week. After we had taken our usual spots on the stoop, Janyce Davis who lives in 1440 pushed her stroller up the walkway. "That your grandbaby?" she asked, stroking her granddaughter's orangeish hair, her smooth cheek. The baby, a child of nearly two, sucked a pacifier contentedly, her huge dark eyes skittering from Limbe to me.

"This here's Isaiah," I said, after a long silence. I stared hard at Janyce, willing her to disappear. She knew damn well that boy wasn't my grandson.

"I hear his Mama calling him in the play yard sometimes," she said. "But I never hear him say nothin' back." She paused and studied Limbe openly. "People say there's something wrong with that boy. Say he's mute or something. Say his daddy beat the words out of him."

Both Limbe and I continued to stare at her evenly, ignoring the cherry ice which had begun to melt through the paper cups. "Nothing wrong with this boy's tongue," I said at last. "Before you came up that walk bothering us, he was telling me a story so long and convoluted, I couldn't hardly follow it. Right, Isaiah?"

But the boy just continued to stare at Janyce. He stared so hard, I knew what he was doing. He was casting his own disappearing spell on her, imagining her and her baby and the carriage going up in one bright cloud of dust. Whoosh!

The small girl in the carriage blinked as if she felt the power of Limbe's spell, then let loose with a fierce howl. But Janyce hardly seemed to notice. She cut the wheels of the carriage so sharp, I was afraid the poor orange-headed girl was going to come tumbling out. When she got to the other side of the parking lot, we heard Janyce cursing that poor baby girl: "Shut-up! You hear me? *Shut the hell up!*"

It was no way to talk to a baby, but the boy and I couldn't help ourselves. We threw our heads back and laughed. Laughed so hard that we forgot about our cherry limbe altogether, and they leaked all over our hands, covering them with stickiness. Laughed so hard that Janyce and her grandbaby heard us from across the parking lot at exactly the same moment. And for a moment, it seemed that everything in the Heights stopped. All the babies stopped crying; and all the Janyces stopped their cursing and screaming and begging for quiet. For a moment it really was quiet. And the noise inside me, the noise that had never been stilled since that night I came home from work and found every window in my house cracked by heat, that stopped too. Or maybe that was just how it seemed to me when I saw Limbe laughing.

Of course, the moment didn't last. It never did. It was cut in half by Cinda, who stepped out of her door and began to call the name I had used when I talked to Janyce. Isaiah. When she saw him sitting on my stoop, her hand fluttered nervously to her mouth, then she began to scold. "What you doing over there? How many times you been told to leave Mrs. Jenkins alone?"

I wanted to tell her it was okay. That I made the limbe for him; I *invited* him to sit on my stoop. But it was no use. She was already apologizing, already tugging him by the hand, already pulling him toward that over-scrubbed apartment where he had learned to hoard up his words.

I shook my head, then went inside and turned on my box. Though I usually keep my music to myself, this time I let it go. I poured Helen Humes out my windows, letting her mingle with my neighbors' salsa, and the pushy beat of that talk-singing. When I looked out across the parking lot, I wondered if anyone in the Heights had ever heard of her. For all I knew, there was no one in the whole world who remembered my favorite singer anymore. No one but me. But as her slinky voice followed me into the kitchen where I was trying to come up with a recipe for coco limbe, I took comfort in Helen's voice, in the way she cried out for love so loud and strong, it had no choice but to come to her.

I sang like that when I thought about Limbe, sang while I scraped coconut on my old grater and mixed it with sugar and water, adding a few drops of cream to make it white. I sang until it was time to light the candles that line my window sill. I tell Junie I light them for the holy souls at my morning funerals, but the truth is I light them for myself. I light them to remind myself the fire that took my babies is still burning. Long as I'm here, that fire lives.

The next day when Limbe arrived at my door with fifteen cents on his palm, I told him his money wouldn't cover the kind of treat I made up the night before. If he wanted one of my special coco limbes, he was going to have to work for it. Smiling wide, he took the can of seed I handed him and followed me to my spot near the dumpster. There we sat on folding chairs and fed the birds who had learned to expect me every day about that hour.

It was a fine day, and whenever one of the doves or chickadees took the seed that Limbe tossed, he pointed excitedly and smiled his pink velvet smile. You wouldn't have thought sitting on folding chairs by the dump feeding birds would have held a boy's attention. But like I said, Limbe had patience. Biblical patience. Maybe it was that name of his, a name I'd begun to like better, the more often I heard it. Though I still wasn't calling him by his Bible name, sometimes I woke up in the middle of the night with it in my mouth. *Isaiah*, I said to myself in a room lit only by my candles for the dead.

Around four Junie came up the hill to show me some new pictures he made. But when he saw Limbe, he stood back. "What's this, Mrs. J.? You got yourself a new friend?"

After he had pulled up a folding chair, making a little sewing circle with me and the boy, I elbowed Limbe. "Don't mind Junie," I said. "He's just a little jealous, that's all."

Junie adjusted his thick rimmed glasses that were held together by a piece of tape, and threw his arm over my shoulder. "Long as you two don't get *too* close," he said.

When Limbe smiled, I could tell he liked Junie the way he liked the birds who came closer and closer to his hand the longer we sat out there in the sun. The way he liked cruising around the parking lot on his plastic trike, or just sitting on my step casting spells on pesky neighbors and watching them disappear.

And Junie liked the boy too. After he had passed one of his drawings to me, he handed it to Limbe, treating him like one of those art critics. The boy studied those pictures carefully, looking from one to the other, then back to the first. When he handed them to Junie, respect mixed with a slight frown on his face. It was exactly how I felt about the pictures. Sure, they were good; all Junie's sketches were. But I disliked the man he had chosen to draw. Disliked his unshaven face and thick jowls, but most of all I disliked his eyes.

"Who is he?" I asked. "Your daddy?"

Junie snatched them from my hand. "Why? You think we look alike?" He held a picture of the ugly stranger up to his own smooth face.

"Sometimes an ugly daddy makes a beautiful son," I said. "And sometimes a beautiful son grows into an ugly daddy. You never know."

It was the kind of talk Junie loved, and he shook his head, and smiled. "Your friend here is a nice lady, but she's a little bit crazy; you know that?" he said to Limbe, winking.

But Limbe only picked up the picture of the jowly old man and grimaced at it, obviously agreeing with me.

"That's Harry," Junie told us, as if making a formal introduction. "My boss at the gas station where I work weekends. He may not have a *nice* face, but it's an interesting one. Look at those eyes."

"You look at them," I said, pushing Harry away. Then after a couple of minutes, I went on. "You know what I think? I think if you make too many pictures of ugly, one morning you gonna look in the mirror and you gonna *be* ugly."

Junie leaned back on two legs of the chair and laughed out loud. "Come on, Mrs. Jenkins! You don't really believe that." He shoved his taped-up glasses back on his nose.

Then the two of us got into one of the long go-nowhere talks we usually have. The kind that make sense to no one but Junie and me. The kind that make Junie practically the only person in the whole project worth talking to.

Course, I thought the boy would be bored. I expected to look up any time and see Limbe running for home. But he kept sitting there, his eyes moving from Junie to me as we spoke, as if our jabbering made more sense than most things he heard. Finally, Junie ran his fingers through the hair that I was always after him to cut, and nudged the boy. "Me and my friend are gettin' hot out here, aren't we, buddy?" He turned to me. "You got anything cold in the fridge, Mrs. J.?"

Well, it was a good thing he mentioned it. After getting lost in a half-hour talk about what makes people turn ugly, I almost forgot about the coco limbe I had promised the boy. Without answering, I started for the apartment, while the two of them lay back in their chairs, taking the summer day into their skin.

When I returned with three limbe in my hands, Junie slapped his leg. "All *right!* Where'd you learn how to make coco limbe, Mrs. J.?"

But after his first lick, he began to shake his head slowly. "Sorry, Mrs. Jenkins, but I think you got to be Puerto Rican to make a good coco limba. It's something that comes down from the mothers, you know?"

"This here's 100 percent American limbe. Not supposed to taste like the Puerto Rican kind," I said, snatching it out of his hand. After I had tossed his on the ground, I stuck out my chin and started on my own. Junie was right: my coco limbe tasted like dishwater laced with coconut, but I wasn't about to let on. I sucked the miserable concoction down to the bottom of the cup.

By then, Junie and I had become like the boy; we had run out of words. The longer we sat, the deeper our quiet got. While I took the opportunity to rest a little from my long walk to a funeral that morning, Limbe concentrated on drawing the birds closer. By then, Junie had taken out his sketchpad and begun to draw the boy. In Junie's drawing, Limbe's face was serious, his hand extended toward the birds. When I noticed the child had hidden his uneaten limba beside his crate, I remembered the cherry-flavored one I had left in the freezer. By then my legs had given in to aching, but I ambled back to the apartment and got it. It was worth it for the light that crossed the boy's face when he saw it in my hand. Limbe may not have talked much, but he had a smile that sang.

By the time I came back, Junie's girlfriend had come out of her apartment in a pair of shorts and a tight T-shirt. It wasn't long before he closed his sketchbook, and told me he'd be around to help me with my groceries on Friday. I thought the boy might go home, too, since we were out of bird seed. But he stayed until his daddy's rattling station wagon pulled into the parking lot.

"Isaiah!" the daddy called sharply, when he spotted the boy sitting on his crate. "What you doing playing by the dumpster?" Immediately, the boy's expression changed to one I had not seen before. Replacing the pink velvet smile was a look I immediately recognized. Forgetting the birds that had mesmerized him, forgetting his half-finished cherry limba, he tossed the cup and ran toward the apartment. When the boy was close enough, the man in the necktie said, "Hasn't your mother told you to stay away from her? Everyone in the Heights knows that old lady's half crazy." He slapped the boy hard on the ass.

Briefly, Limbe looked back at me, his face twisted into his mother's sorry look.

He wasn't crying, but when I closed my eyes I could hear the howl just the same. It was like the one inside me, the one I tried to drown out with music every morning at strangers' funerals. When he continued to stare at me, I yelled out to him, "You heard your daddy. You stay away from me. You come to my door anymore I'll call the police on you." It was a ridiculous threat to make against a four-year-old. But since most people thought I was crazy, I figured I had license to say what I wanted.

Immediately, I ran into the house and slammed the door so hard that its cheap hinges rattled. Then I pressed my back against it, like someone was after me, though I wasn't sure who or what I thought I was keeping out. At first I thought it was the man choking on his necktie who called me crazy, and who slapped the words out of his son. But then I realized it wasn't him at all. No, it was the boy who scared me. Limbe. Isaiah. It was the silent howl that had crossed the parking lot, almost knocking me over with its force. Like Janyce, I had yelled in a way no one should ever talk to a child, but the truth was I couldn't help it.

Inside my apartment, I made a lot of noise throwing out all the failed coco limbe I had made, getting rid of the 500 Dixie cups I had bought, tossing out packs of Kool-Aid. "No limbe here, boy. Don't come knockin' on this door. Didn't you hear your daddy? The lady in this apartment is crazy. Possessed. Out of her mind." And as I scoured the apartment of everything that reminded me of that child, working with the kind of energy I hadn't felt for years, I truly felt that I was.

* * *

You would have thought my mean words and his father's slap would have been enough to keep the boy away, but the very next day I heard his bird-pecking at my door. However, this time, no amount of patience, biblical or otherwise, was going to outlast me. I wasn't answering the door if the boy stood out there till puberty overtook him. He waited on my step a good hour, pausing for several minutes, then beginning his noise again. "Limbe?" he called through my open window, his voice mournful and determined all at once.

After he was gone, I yelled at the silent door. "What you want, sitting around with some old lady and her American dishwater limbe? You should be playing out in the playground with the rest of them. You should be talking, *yelling!* Do you hear me! You should be telling the whole world your name. Like Helen Humes did. Like those talk singers do. Make them learn it good!"

Isaiah's patience lasted exactly as long as summer. But once the air turned crisp, he stopped coming. It was almost as if the only thing he really wanted had been those limbe.

Since I never saw him on the plastic trike anymore, I wondered if the family had moved. But then I noticed Cinda toting her laundry across the parking lot. And one night when I couldn't sleep, I spotted a cruiser pulling up outside their apartment. I immediately snapped my shades shut.

Whatever their problem was, it was none of my business. And when Junie tried to talk to me about it, I told him so. I told him that boy was nothing to me; I had already forgotten him. I told him the last thing I needed was some child who never talked bothering my life. But Junie just clucked and nodded in a way I found particularly irritating. In fact, I found it so irritating, I told him to get out; I didn't need him coming around here either. Him and his beautiful drawings of ugly people. I'm lucky Junie doesn't take me too serious, because I don't now how I'd drag my groceries home if he didn't show up regularly on Fridays. But after that, he knew better than to talk to me about the boy.

* * *

It may be true my mind is gone, probably *is* true, but I know something that most people don't. I know that Life has a way of breaking each one of us. I'm not talking about the general things that happen: old age, and the smell of sick, and loss piled on loss. I'm talking about a breaking that's specific to each person. Sirens are mine. Though I wasn't there to hear them that night when my house burned up, I've been listening to them every night since.

Was it any accident that the only housing my caseworker could find for me was here in the Heights? Here in this place where I spend my days and nights listening to the sirens that rush to this project every day of the year? Police, ambulances, and every now and then even a fire truck, though usually for nothing. Some kid desperate to make something happen who pulls the alarm. Then there was the time Melissa in 5150 shorted out her toaster and caught her curtains on fire. And some years ago, Ida Healey set a serious blaze in 1221. Fortunately, the only one who got hurt was the old drunk herself. And most people said the burning did her good. It burned away her craving for drink forever.

But on this particular day, the fire was real. Small, yes. Contained, yes. But very real. I was walking home from a funeral for a retarded man, muttering about how poor the turnout had been. Maybe even thinking how pathetic my own might be. After all, who would come? Junie? That girlfriend of his, probably showing up in one of her short skirts, wild hair not even properly combed? In fact, I was so lost in my own funeral dirge that, for once, I hardly noticed the sirens. Didn't even realize I had heard them until I saw the two vehicles outside the apartment where Isaiah lived. There was the fire truck, of course, but I was looking at the ambulance. The ambulance that was gaping open like a mouth, prepared to swallow somebody up.

As usual, there was a crowd around the trouble, people lined up with their kids in front of them so even the youngest wouldn't miss any of the misery. The crowd was so thick that I couldn't see much. Course, I started praying right away, hoping that it was Isaiah's father who'd be carried out on the stretcher. Or even Cinda. Cinda hiding her face, and apologizing to the crowd for making such a spectacle. But somewhere in me I knew it was Limbe. Even before I heard the words that passed through the crowd like a game of telephone, I knew.

"Playing with one of those disposable lighters," people said. "His mama asleep on the couch while her shows hummed in the background." Oh yes, they were nodding and buzzing, murmuring about how it wouldn't happen to *their* kids. About how they never left a lighter around where the kids could get at it. Never fell asleep in the middle of the day. Only when the paramedics came out with the stretcher did the buzzing stop.

I still couldn't get close enough to see the boy, but I saw Cinda's face as clear as anything. Saw that it had been washed clean of everything she had been before. It was the face I had worn every single day since that night I came home late from work. And before I knew what I was doing, I was moving through the crowd, pushing babies out of my way, elbowing their nosy mothers. All I knew was that I had to get a glimpse of the boy, had to see his face, had to know what was in his eyes. But as I pushed my way to the front, I forgot where I was. By the time I reached him, I half expected to see my own boy being loaded on that ambulance, not some neighbor child who had never said more than *coco limbe* to me. In my confusion, I even began to call my son's name. "Michael! *Michael!*" It was a name I hadn't said out loud in decades.

But before I could get near the ambulance, Cinda stopped me. With a ferocity I never suspected she had in her, she pushed me back hard. If the crowd hadn't been behind me, I would have landed right on my ass.

"What are you saying? That's not *Michael!*" she shouted. "Crazy old woman, you stay away from my baby!"

But it wasn't her strength that stopped me. It was her eyes. Hard as onyx, they stared out at me from her washed clean face. And right then and there I realized that she knew. Knew it was my fault. Knew that somehow by feeding that boy, by sitting with him, by drawing out his smile, I had pulled him into my fire. *I had made it happen.*

* * *

That night the crazy in me went on a rampage. I batted all the candles that line my window sill off their waxy perch. Who was I to think I could talk back to fire? Dare it to come for me? Then I took out my best red dress, the one I save for funerals, and began to cut it up with a pair of scissors. *Stay away from here!* I yelled so loud that the Bonillas tapped on the thin wall that separates us, warning me to be quiet. Who I was talking to, I don't know. Maybe to the boy who had waited on my step through the summer, calling out for limbe. Or to Michael, who had come back more vivid than he'd been in years. Or maybe I was talking to fire itself. *Don't you come any closer, you hear?*

For three days I stayed in my apartment, hiding from the neighborhood talk. I didn't want to know the details of Limbe's clash with fire, especially didn't want to hear what happened after they carried him away in that ambulance. Anyway, there was no need to go out. I was through with strangers' funerals, through with the noisy birds who gathered at the dumpster waiting for me. When I opened the fridge on Friday, I realized I had eaten so little I didn't even need to go to the grocery store. With any luck, I'd never have to go again.

When Junie knocked on the door at our usual Friday time, I pretended I wasn't home. But he was like the boy; he didn't take silence for an answer. Instead, he banged harder. "Come on, Mrs. J., I know you're in there. Open up." And when that didn't work, he went from window to window, pushing his face into the glass, rapping hard with his knuckles. "What do I gotta do to make sure you're still breathin' in there?" he called. "Get the police over here? Cause I will, Mrs. J.; you know I will."

That's when I sprung open the door. "Didn't your grandmother ever teach you manners?" I looked a fright. No make-up. Still in my bathrobe. Hair not even done up.

But Junie didn't seem to notice. "She taught me manners all right. And I use them at the right times. Now isn't one of them." He pushed through the door and shoved a scrap of paper into my hand. It was covered with his own dramatic handwriting: *St. Mark's Hospital. Room 208.*

"What's this supposed to be?" I crumpled the paper into a ball.

"Listen, Mrs. J., I don't claim to know how you're feeling. Or what you're thinking. But I do know if you don't go see that boy, you're gonna end up as crazy as people say you are. Now come on and get dressed; I'll drive."

"Nothin' wrong with crazy. Sometimes crazy's the last

place on earth left to go." I pulled my bathrobe around me tighter and squinted at him.

"Yeah, maybe it is. But not for you. If it was, you would have taken that route long ago." He pushed me toward my bedroom. "Come on now, get dressed. And I want you in something nice, too. Something with matching shoes and pocketbook, the way you usually look."

After I had bathed and done my hair, I stood looking in my closet for half an hour before I found something I hadn't worn to a funeral. I could hear Junie's fingers strumming on various surfaces as he moved around my living room. Finally I came up with an old housedress with lavender flowers splattered across it. Though it wasn't up to my standards for public visiting, it was the only thing I hadn't worn in the presence of a dead body. I pulled it over my head, then decorated it up with a purple necklace, and a pair of sky blue shoes. They weren't the right shade—not even close, but they would have to do.

When I presented myself to Junie he sized me up. "Now that's more like it," he said, smiling like a new beau.

But I just waved him out of my way. "Come on, if we're doing this, we're doing it quick—before I have time to think on it much."

But as it turned out, the ten-minute ride to the hospital was too much time. A couple of times we stopped at a light, and I put my hand on the door, tempted to bolt. When we reached the hospital parking lot, Junie said, "Up the elevator and turn right. 208's the fourth room on the left."

But by then I felt as small and stubborn as the boy who had appeared at my door in the beginning of the hot season. "Not today, Junie. Maybe I'll come back tomorrow" I said, clinging to the door handle. "I mean, I can't hardly go up there without bringing the boy a gift, can I?"

For once, Junie looked at me like other people did. "It's your choice," he said, sounding real cold. Leaning across me, he pushed my door open. "You want to go up and see the boy, I'll wait. Otherwise, it's a fifteen-mile hike back to the Heights."

"You wouldn't do that to me, Junie," I said in a voice that embarrassed me with its frailty. "You know these old legs would never—"

But Junie wasn't buying. "To tell you the truth, Mrs. Jenkins, I'm tired of worrying about what you do. Matter of fact, right now I'm tired of you altogether. You and your whole damn tragic life." He looked toward the sidewalk and began his familiar strumming, apparently waiting for me to climb out and start hiking.

"Just because I want to wait till tomorrow—" I began, but again Junie cut me off.

"How long since that fire killed your family?" he asked, staring me right in the face, not a speck of mercy in his eyes.

"Twenty-seven years," I said. My voice had gone to a whisper.

"Then for twenty-seven years you've been walking around thinking everything that happened was about you and that fire. Why should tomorrow be any different?"

Well, that did it. By then I actually thought I could walk that fifteen miles, no problem. But when I moved to get out of his car, Junie grabbed my arm. And when I looked up at him, I saw the softness that nothing on earth could keep out of his eyes. "Don't you get it, Mrs. J?" he said, his voice as low as mine. "This isn't about you. This has nothing to do with what happened in your house twenty-seven years ago. This is about Isaiah. A boy who everyone expects to recover and be just fine—if you're interested."

It took me a minute to hear through all the anger I had built up around me, but finally Junie's words got through. "Did you say the boy was gonna be fine?" I said clutching his wrist so tight I left my claw marks on it. "Are you sure? Why the hell didn't you tell me that before?"

In answer, Junie just sat back and smiled. "I wanted to let him tell you himself. He's been asking for you, you know."

"For *me*?" I reared up and clutched my purse. "Why would a boy who never once said my name out loud call for me?"

"I didn't say he called you by name, did I? But then you two never had much use for names."

I blinked at the almost blinding brightness in Junie's dark eyes.

"Anyway, he *did* ask for you. Cinda told me herself," he continued. "In fact, you were the first one he called when he opened his eyes that day after the fire. 'Limbe,' he whispered. And when none of the nurses knew what in hell he was talking about, he raised his voice louder. 'Limbe!' he shouted as if he wanted to wake every soul that was slumbering or quietly dying in that hospital. 'Limbe! Limbe! Limbe!'"

* * *

Patry Francis has been published in The Ontario Review, The Massachusetts Review, Prairie Schooner, *and numerous other journals. New stories are forthcoming in* Tampa Review *and* Colorado Review. *Currently, she is working on a novel.*

Vasilis Afxentiou
Etude

from The Rose & Thorn Literary E-zine

———————————— • ————————————

I lianna didn't wake Dino up, but brought with her a mug of Nescafe' and settled in the chair. The pungency of the black brew briefly dispersed the sleepiness in her head.

She had heard the melody one day in the past. But today her fingers felt thick, clumsy, undisciplined. The tips were blistered on her left hand and her thumb cramped from fatigue.

"How are your exercises proceeding?" Anastasi had asked her at the music conservatory the other day, giving her a pat as she stretched the knotted muscles of her back.

"Just fine."

He had looked at her with those knowing eyes, weighing and regarding, as he stood in front of her, twice attempting to say something that he did not.

She enjoyed watching his curiously delicate manner. He used his large hazel eyes to tell more than his tongue—but that morning she pretended to busy herself preparing, not looking at him for long, for she knew he was probing her. She had even evaded their usual patter.

"You're not well?" He had finally acquiesced.

"Not very. It'll pass."

He put the stool and foot rest in place, shifted ebulliently with brisk, spirited movement. And he paused a little. He did not sit immediately, but delayed this moment of focus. He relinquished himself to it as thoroughly as to his playing. He was never hurried at this particular stage; he never rushed at this point. It was, she thought, a kind of liturgy in him, just as when he was performing, he was undividedly surrendering.

Yet Anastasi could be as utterly grave or severe. His

reproaches were the bleakest she had ever seen. He taught as an evangelist preached. It was for this thoroughness, she imagined, that she felt esteem for him.

Ilianna now raised the instrument off her lap and laid it upright next to a desk scattered with music sheets, a copy of Chosen Country by J. dos Passos, and Mary Magdalene portrayed weeping.

She heard Dino get up and she shut her eyes. The tiny garret closed in on her and a sudden vortex made her slump to one side. She caught herself from falling and sprung her slight, lean torso up straight on the uncomfortable chair. Two years, Anastasi had said. Two hard years for the fingers to break in.

"Don't give up," was his favourite infamous statement. "You come to me with a perfect right hand."

She whiffed the heavy blue smoke meandering into her cubbyhole study from the Gauloises Dino was smoking in the kitchen. Her throat tightened and her nostrils pinched. He was making Greek coffee. Its rich fragrance mingled, somewhere along the way, with the silty wafts from his cigarette. The smells made her head whirl. Oblivious to her discomfort she could hear him singing, " Take my hand/Take my whole life too . . ." To him— the King was The King.

She sat there listening and stared at the only two paintings in the apartment. One was an Andrew Wyeth and the other a Norton Simon. They represented her wealth and were a gift from her mother, who had brought them from Astoria, Long Island, six months after Ilianna had departed from her home.

She had been raised in the ancient neighbourhood of Plaka, in a house of post-classical architecture that vaunted better days right after the war. Her family was moderately wealthy, an old Athenian family, endorsing the old ways, trying hard not to be assimilated by the onrush of world changes fostered by satellite television and her media-nurtured generation. From childhood she had known that her future was already planned out. She would be sent to college, earn her degree, and marry a man with a solid profession, perhaps even a shipowner. But all that had changed when one morning she left her home with rucksack bearing down on her thin shoulders and trust in a calling.

> *And I will love thee still, my dear,*
> *Till a' the seas gang dry:*
> *Till a' the seas gang dry, my dear,*
> *And the rocks melt wi' the sun;*

came the Burns' hyperbole in the form of a TV commercial for scotch whisky from the kitchen where Dino sat.

They had been together for almost a year, since she was nineteen and he twenty-three. He was like nobody she had ever met before. He didn't worry any more about the years ahead than did cattle in green pastures. There was a primal manner in his air and a puerile spontaneity that uninhibited her. He had a careering way about him, like a twentieth century gladiator: all was intense sport, lovemaking, drinking, prancing his shiny secondhand Harley as if he were Marlon Brando and she the counter waitress.

His family had been killed in a train disaster when he was four. He had been on his own since he was twelve, when he had done away with the source of his obstacles by hurtling himself over a glass-strewn wall. The opportunity had come, just before Christmas dawn. Another inmate and he had scaled the shard-sowed barrier to freedom, bloodied and frostbitten. Nightmares of the orphanage persisted to this day.

A garage owner had offered him a job and Dino had taken his courage in both hands. Though he was still a boy then, he grew up fast to become a man. Yet the strong arms transformed to comforting wings at night. She could have let her life surrender into his and part with all that tortured her, walk away from her own honeyed trial, into the tangy freedom his world promised . . .

The guitar stood waiting. Elegant, skillfully crafted, painful, it ignored her musings and the fever in her hands. Two years had passed four months ago, and still her appendages moved slowly, sluggishly, producing a cacophony. There were days when she played adeptly, but few. She could not account for it.

Dino's deep, black eyes were upon her from where he sat, this minute. She could feel their moot, fixed look. It had been a bad night, last night. A bad night for love. There had been depression in the dark of the room, a tiredness she felt more often than not. He had finally left her and gone to the other end of the bed, and she had lain alone and silent. Sirocco-warm tears ebbed out of her scouring the hours by.

The night faded once more whence it came. She massaged the thumb muscle to lessen the stiffness. Veins stood out like winding blue worms on her forearm and the back of her hand. Dipping her fingers into the dish of alcohol temporarily numbed them.

Her index finger puffed out at the bottom, tapering like an obelisk of flesh to a firm phalanx. A straight dark line of clotted blood scarred the once soft tissue behind the finger nail. Friction from the repeated barre exercises maintained the wound, fresh and visible. All were the credits of the craft. All the visible signs of hard, diligent work were there. Texture was not.

Dino brushed by her on his way out. She smelled the tobacco on his clothes. He stood by the door not speaking, then closed it behind him.

"The classical guitar is like a man," had been Anastasi's first words that decisive March noon. Ilianna's first lesson had begun.

"He will want and want some more. You will hate and love him. Give yourself to him and he will give everything to you. As someone once said, 'Love is, above all, the gift of oneself'."

Anastasi had then embraced the guitar and began to play

the 'etude. Ilianna's last minute doubts dissolved with certainty. Each undulating stroke charged a longing that had so long been left yearning for its mate. The cords mingled and blended, entwined and braided, melded and plexed and fused, weaving a dulcet onomatopoeia of counterpoint plenishing her every pore, progressing so ever-softly turning, spinning sheer summer air into a gossamer completion that longingly never came. The tinkling of the strings echoed, ignoring, conquering time.

"'The moan of doves in immemorial elms/And murmuring of innumerable bees'—do you hear him, do you hear Maestro Tennyson's sigh in the pluckings? You are in love, no?" Anastasi had remarked, putting the guitar down.

"Yes."

But the instrument before her seemed unconcerned, aloof, like Dino. Both promised ecstasy, both wanted her soul. But she had not the strength to serve two masters.

When she had awakened it was a comfort to know that the entire day would belong to her alone. But by the time she got through the Segovia scales, even the light burden of the instrument was too much for her to hold. She had not slept much during the night, she realized, for her eyelids drooped more often than not. She had a drifty feeling that made her dreamlike and lose herself.

"Rest if you must, but don't you quit," came Cushing's words from the poem Anastasi had drilled into her memory two years before.

Finally, she put the guitar down. The noon sun rays dabbed the wall next to her with a craggy segment of column from the Parthenon beyond. She found herself gliding into oblivion on the chair. She dozed. She was overwhelmed by her dreaming of her mother and felt happiness.

She was seldom like this, not ever since they had met. But now, like a torrent, the cumulated snags in their relationship suddenly all deluged upon her, and she was surprised that she did nothing to stop the onset. She recollected afresh their quarrel the night before, recalled the options remaining, put to her. About the music—she could not remember what had been said to be wrong with it. Possibly it was not the music; she did not know. She retained only the oppressive, mostly mute, suffocation of Dino's demands.

At the recollection she began to tremble for an instant, uncontrollably, and gasp for more air to enter her lungs. It had been a turbulent episode, the worst; like an Aegean August gale, with only a hint of warning, that drowns one unsuspectingly. She was sinking, she told herself. She was feeble against his wants—whatever these were. And perhaps the giving on her part would never quench the needing on his . . .

Her fingers felt better. She dipped them once more and waited for them to dry. The melody came again, this time urging and stronger than before. She picked up the guitar and gave, yielding herself to it. There was a knock on the door that she did not hear.

She was solely aware that the mellifluous pluckings did not come from the instrument but from her. Like heartbeats, they were as much hers as her heart's. A presence was there, completing her metamorphosis. Unlike before, she knew, the threshold now was scaled, the union of her self and her dream realized. She played, all of her, and did not stop her care because now she could not. Like the pulsing in her chest, her will no longer participated in its existence. A being had been freed, and free, it reigned over a kingdom of two. The knocking stopped. The footsteps died softly away behind the closed door, and the room glowed in the summer afternoon with Ilianna and a sublime 'etude.

* * *

Vasilis Afxentiou was born in Thessaloniki, Greece. He attended Norwalk State College and Old Dominion University in the United States where he received his degrees. He is a teacher of English as a Second Language and English as a Foreign Language in Athens, Greece. He has been teaching English part-time since

1968, and full-time since 1985. He also majored in the classical guitar at the Hellenic Conservatory. Vasilis's writing credits include published fiction and nonfiction in Greece, Europe, Australia, Canada and in the USA. His writing includes articles and essays, a theatrical play, five novels, a novella, and a book of short stories. He is a candidate to be published in the poetry anthology of CONTEMPORARY GREEK POETS, VOL. III.

Patricia Hackbarth

A Brief
Geological Guide
To Canyon Country

from The Georgia Review

———————————— • ————————————

Anticline: An upward arching of rock strata caused by pressure from underneath, which severely fractures the upper surface and promotes erosion.

When my father returned from Korea in 1951, long before I was born, he didn't go directly home to the family in New Hampshire that was so anxious to see him safe and sound. Instead he stopped off with one of his army buddies in Moab, Utah. His friend's father was living in a trailer there and mining uranium, hoping to get rich. The two young men spread out their army blankets on the cramped floor at night, and went exploring in the wild and strange landscape during the day, hiking and hitching rides.

My father, a famously silent man, never spoke of what he saw. I know from my grandmother that he extended his stay several times, finally returning after three months of her growing impatience with the delay and with his failure to explain it.

Over the forty-odd years that followed, he met my mother at a church supper, produced five children, labored on a road-building crew operating heavy machinery, buried my mother when she succumbed to a liver tumor, finished raising the five of us without ever talking about her illness, and only twice mentioned his travels in Utah.

The first time was when my oldest sister brought an art project home from school. It was an abstract pastel, horizontal and diagonal strokes breached here and there by a vertical plunge, in a terra-cotta shade with a few darker streaks. Dad looked at it with far more interest than he usually spared for her high school artworks, and finally said, "It reminds me of Utah." My sister had no idea what he meant, but she was immensely pleased when he hung the picture on the kitchen cupboard.

It stayed there for five days, and during that time I saw him pause more than once, while frying potatoes or washing out the coffeepot, to study it. When we came home from school on the fifth day and found the cupboard door empty, my sister asked him where the picture was. "It's in your room," he said. We knew him well enough to know that was all the answer she would get.

The second time was late this past winter, after Colin, the man I'd loved and lived with for four years, decided he wanted something else, something he couldn't quite identify but that in any case wasn't me. Colin was a man of boundless interests and an insatiable need to talk about them. For every sentence my dad withheld, Colin supplied twelve. He spent entire evenings telling me how ants communicate, how art forgeries are detected, why ice expands when it freezes, how steel is made, how the Enigma machine broke the Nazi code. His eyes were the color of light, and they burned with a luminous intensity as he talked, his eyes and his talk filling up my emptiness. In all that volume of words I never heard *I'm not happy, I want something else.* Maybe I just missed it. Maybe I was better at listening to silence.

My dad, for all his taciturnity, was not an unfeeling man, and he offered me his large and silent company, many evenings in a row when necessary, until I could get my feet back under me. On one of those evenings, while the TV flickered with the sound turned off and I pretended to read in my mom's old rocker, he said, "You ought to take a trip out to Utah."

I looked up in surprise. "Utah? Why?"

He shrugged and looked uncomfortable, as if he hadn't expected to have to explain. "You could learn something there," he said at last. I waited to hear what it was I might learn, what he thought I needed just then, but he'd gone back to watching the TV.

At that point in my life, with the nights blacker than black and the ground heading off in unpredictable directions under my feet, I was ready to try anything. "Suppose we both go," I said.

After a moment he turned toward me, his eyes pensive, focused on the distance. "I'll think about that," he said.

Two weeks later he had a massive coronary. I don't know what the gravely ill think about amidst the tubes and dials and hardware, whether they relive vital events or long for their loved ones or contemplate the vastness of eternity. I don't know if his sojourn in the desert, so crucial early in his life, was something he reflected on at the end. He'd kept his thoughts close for seventy years, and he took them with him when he left.

Joint: A fracture in one or more layers of rock, without displacement; water seeping into the joint hastens the process of erosion.

Approaching Moab from the east, the highway shares the canyon with the Colorado River for several miles. It's here that I pull off to survey the massive horizontal slabs of the canyon wall, the raw vertical cuts, the talus that has been lying in suspended calamity on the slope for how many thousands of years, sheared away from its moorings and destined to spend nearly forever in its fall.

It's not really red, this rock in the setting sun; it's some shade of orange, salmon or coral or vermilion. But it's also the color of a steel mill at night, of a scalded lobster, of seared earth, bringing questions of survival to mind.

As the sun sinks closer to the rim, the colors pool in the hollows, drawing into themselves. Perhaps gods have always lived on mountaintops; colors, I've just discovered, live in the indentations in rock. Is that what it was, I ask my father, who I hope has made the trip out here with me in some form. Was it that frozen fire?

I get out of the car and lean against it and watch the show, while time and the occasional vehicle pass behind me. After a few minutes or an hour I notice the sound of an engine idling close by. I turn to see an ancient blue Land Cruiser pulled up alongside my car, the driver leaning across the seat to roll down the passenger window. "Are you having car trouble?" he asks.

I shake my head, then by way of explanation gesture toward the rock. "It's red."

His eyes flick over in that direction as if to double-check, then he says slowly, "Right."

"I mean *really* red. I mean . . . maybe this is nothing to you, but I haven't ever seen anything like it."

He looks back up at the canyon wall and so do I, and then he shuts off the engine. He gets out of the truck and comes and stands next to my car, hands in his jeans pockets, head tilted to the side as he surveys the rock. He's fortyish and rangy, chunks of dark hair falling over his forehead, cautious eyes. "Usually the tourists go on into the parks and look at the really impressive stuff," he says.

I wince a little at the word "tourist," but I say, "This isn't impressive?"

He studies me for a moment, much as he'd studied the canyon wall, then begins to tell me about the different types of sandstone, about flood plains and coastal lagoons, layering and erosion, uplifts and fractures, siltstone and mudstone and color-banded shale, the violence and the unimaginable time that went into the sculpting of the landscape. Then he breaks off in the middle of a sentence and says, "This is probably boring."

"Boring!" I look at him in astonishment. It would never have occurred to Colin that he could bore me. I shake my head and add, "You sure do know your neighborhood."

"It's pretty hard to live here without wanting to know how it got this way," he says.

I decide to tell him about my father, though there isn't much to tell. He listens, and looks more thoughtful than a man usually does when hearing about a stranger, then studies the river in silence for a few moments and finally recommends a bookstore in Moab that has a geology section. "Good luck with your search," he says, and seems to mean it, as he gets back in his truck and drives off.

By now the sun has dipped behind the rim and the shadows are smoothing over the rough edges on rock and river, and all I've eaten today was the corn muffin on the first flight and the peanuts on the second, and I haven't a clue where I'm going to sleep tonight, so I climb back into my car and head for town.

I find an inexpensive motel and check in for a week. The desk clerk is a young woman with a mass of curly red hair and a dozen silver bracelets, each of which rings on a different pitch. I know this because she plays tunes on them while I fill out the form. Along with the room key she offers me local brochures, wakeup calls, and glazed doughnuts. I settle for the brochures, and she hopes I have a "great night," as if people come to Moab for the nightlife.

With my stomach rumbling I toss my suitcase in the room and head for the joint across the street, whose pink and blue sign keeps flashing its news of burgers and pizza and ice cream. I toil my way through a tough-crusted pizza while a woman on the jukebox sings about her dog being better company than the guy who jilted her. Then I head back across the road under a parachute of stars dimmed by neon.

My courage deserts me once I'm back in my room. It's just me and a faded blue bedspread and a TV with a cigarette burn in the veneer. The sign outside may say No Vacancy but this room right here is the emptiest one in Moab.

I grab the ice bucket and stride across the parking lot to the office. The clerk is playing solitaire with the radio turned down low. She says "How y'all doing," and I say fine and dump some change in the vending machine and return to my room with a Dr. Pepper, trying to fit some of it into the little plastic cup in the bathroom. Then I turn on a sitcom, but it won't do.

I hurry back outside and look for a place to take a walk. First I make a circuit around the motel; but there's broken glass in back, and two people peek out from behind their curtains to see who's prowling around. So I walk up and down the road for awhile, breathing deeply, trying to inhale the serenity of the stars; when I get tired of that I get my desk chair and plant it on the little apron of concrete in front of my door and sit there, waiting to get sleepy.

After awhile the motel sign goes off, followed by the light in the office, leaving just a dim night light glowing in some distant corner. The redhead comes out and locks the door and walks into the parking lot, jingling her keys, when she suddenly notices me sitting there in the dark. She seems startled at first, then looks at me more closely. "You've got yourself a busted-up love affair, haven't you?" she says.

I burst into tears. This is the last thing I intended to do. She hunts through her purse for tissues, hands me one. She's looking for more while I blow my nose, and I say, "I'm okay. Really."

"You sure?" She sits down on the fender of my car, her jeans so tight she can barely bend her knees. I think she'd be better off without all those doughnuts; but I'm instantly contrite.

"Guess I can recognize that well enough," she says. "My boyfriend lived off me for two years while he couldn't find a job, and then as soon as he got something he split. I saw him a week later with a new girlfriend. It would help if I could hate him, but I don't." She tells it calmly, though her voice drops a bit on the last sentence. I murmur something sympathetic. She shrugs and says, "If there's one thing that's for sure, it's that you just can't count on people too much. But what else have we got?"

I look over to where the Moab Rim rears up along the west side of the highway, gathering the stars as they drift slowly into it. I want to imagine its massive presence as benign, even protective.

She gets up, dusts off her jeans. "I'm Tracy, and I come on every night at eight. If you get feeling rotten, just come on over."

I watch the taillights of her car as she drives away, then take a few more breaths of the desert night, preparing to face the blue bedspread.

Fins: Thin, upright slabs of rock formed by fracture of the strata by anticlines and subsequent erosion of the joints.

At the bookstore I arm myself with guidebooks, histories, and a geological dictionary, as much to keep myself busy at night as to instruct myself during the day, and go off to see the world. On the first day I see sandstone arches, a collared lizard, petrified sand dunes, huge rocks balanced impossibly on slender pedestals, a fox disappearing into the grama grass, and an old log cabin that is vying with the arches to see which of them collapses first. On the second day I see a canyon so vast that I forget to breathe, a bighorn sheep with her baby, a claret cup cactus, sandstone spires standing like a great dead stone city, juniper trees covered with blue-green berries, mesas and buttes and fins and all the empty spaces between them, a tree trunk that has been twisted two full turns like a corkscrew, and the confluence of two great rivers down near what seems like the center of the earth—rivers placid looking from the rim but deceptively violent, clearly the victors in their ageless battle with the rock.

In the evenings I browse in the shops, then eat at Wrangler Rick's, where the kitchen is open until midnight, returning to my room with as much of the night gone as possible. At Wrangler Rick's it's noisy around the bar, but there are booths in back where I can eat in relative peace and eavesdrop on the conversations around me, borrowing other people's lives for awhile.

On the second night, as I'm finishing my tacos, I spot Mr. Blue Land Cruiser sitting alone in a nearby booth. He's absorbed in his own thoughts, and doesn't look as if he wants to be disturbed. But he sees me a moment later, nods, hesitates, then gets up and comes over. "Want company, or—?"

"Please," I say with my mouth full, then swallow without chewing, wishing I had at least brushed my hair. "I have so many questions for you!"

He looks startled, then laughs. "Like what?"

"Like why do some layers of rock erode straight up and down, while others crumble into pyramids? And how do those trees get so twisted? And how—" I stop, afraid I must sound idiotic.

He goes back for his food, then sits down across from me. His mouth is still amused but his eyes get serious. He does his best to answer my questions and then others, his enchiladas getting cold while he talks; I miss some of what he says because I'm so grateful to have my questions taken seriously. Maybe there's something in it for him, too; the weighty thoughts that seemed to oppress him lift when he talks about the land. His hands move expertly to illustrate the structure of various types of rock, and he seems to come out of himself far enough to hope for something, though perhaps he knows more about sandstone than about what he hopes for.

Along the way he tells me his name is Nat. He teaches the history of science in Salt Lake and spends the rest of his time here reading and working on a book about mass extinctions, and he lives south of town in a house with a view of the La Sal Mountains and the Book Cliffs.

"The Book Cliffs," I say. "Are they the ones to the north that seem to go on forever?"

He nods. "I like to hike under the rim, with that huge presence on one side of me. It's sort of reassuring. Which is funny, when you're walking on the rubble that proves how impermanent it all really is . . . " He looks out toward the neon reflecting off the fender of a truck, and the rest of his thought leaks soundlessly into the night. He brings himself back with an effort and says, "What about you?"

I tell him that my name is Janis and I teach college too, which is why I'm out here in May before the tourists arrive; my subject is twentieth-century history, taught from a variety of viewpoints. "But," I add, "all this practice with other people's perspectives hasn't helped me understand much of what my father thought about anything." Or Colin, I add silently.

He's quiet while he works on his dinner, then he asks, "What happened to him in Korea?"

I shake my head. "That's another thing we don't know. He never talked about that, either."

He looks disappointed. "A weather-and-sports man then?"

"Not even that. He just didn't talk, period." I picture my father as I always have: broad-shouldered with big arms and a round face, deep-set gray eyes that may have taken plenty in, a small mouth that never let any of it out. "My grandfather, my dad's father, died while Dad was over there. My grandmother wrote and told him, of course. After awhile he wrote back and asked what the headstone looked like. That was all. My grandmother said his letters got even shorter after that. One paragraph cramped up at the top of the page, the rest empty. She figured all that blank space was the stuff he wanted to say but couldn't."

He nods and pushes his plate back, sips his coffee. "At least you had a talkative grandmother."

"Yes, I did." I think of all the things she used to confide in me as we baked bread or darned socks or husked corn on the back porch, speaking to me as if I were an adult and would understand, and suddenly I miss her all over again and my eyes start to fill.

"Whoops," he says.

Cap Rock: A hard, relatively impervious layer of rock overlying a softer one such as shale. The cap rock provides some protection to the softer layer and delays erosion.

Nat has suggested some hiking trails, and with topo map in hand I set out to investigate them. The first one leads to an overlook with a slice of river visible between two buttes deep in the canyon. Under the rim a pinyon pine grips a bare sprinkling of soil in a narrow crevice, growing improbably out of a nearly unbroken rock face, its needles clustered like fists. Overhead swifts and swallows ride the updrafts, reeling and diving and rising again, making the air visible, its currents sculpting it like the rock beneath.

High above there are broken clouds and a steady breeze pushing them along. I watch the shadows move against the canyon walls, the surface constantly transformed, the colors ever changing. When the shadows recede, a layer of rock seems to fall away, the skin peeling from the body of the earth.

I imagine my father down on the canyon floor, a small lone figure raising a faint veil of dust as he tramps through the arid landscape like an old desert prospector. I wish I could call out to him, ask him what he's looking for here.

The next day I follow a trail along the rim of a deep and narrow canyon that empties into a deeper one still, the rims of other side canyons lined up beyond it like the lobes of an oak leaf until they vanish into the haze, the closest I've come to infinity. The silence is terrifying and alluring. It's not the silence of an abandoned railroad siding or a street blanketed with late-night snow, but the naked silence of the universe, the silence of my house with the roof come off and the emptiness radiating to the farthest part of the sky. The silence of nothing. I ask my father, Was that it? Was it the silence? But he is silent too.

I lie on my stomach on the brink with my head hanging down, listening, feeling myself expand into all that space. This posture eventually brings some excited attention from the next party of hikers to happen along, a troop of Boy Scouts who think I've fallen and may be dead or at least in a coma. They're all ready to earn a first-aid badge, and are visibly disappointed when I sit up. "I'm just listening to the canyon," I tell their crew-cut leader, who has plainly decided I'm odd and leads his charges away.

I see Nat at Wrangler Rick's again in the evening, and I begin to wonder if he's also warding off the night. This time he comes over and sits down without an invitation. I tell him what I've been up to since I saw him last, hazarding a remark or two about the fearsome silence. He nods knowingly. Then I mention the Boy Scouts and their puzzled leader, which makes him laugh. He tells me where I might spot golden eagles and turkey vultures, then mentions a trail that a high-clearance vehicle can negotiate. I tell him my rental car can barely manage the potholes in the motel parking lot. He recollects he hasn't got anything to do on Sunday, so why doesn't he drive me. I recollect (but don't mention) that I do have something to do on Sunday, and that's fly home—but I've been thinking about extending my stay.

Arch: A natural opening in a fin or other thin wall of rock created when one portion of the wall erodes more quickly than the surrounding area.

At first I have my doubts whether any sort of wheeled contraption could negotiate some of the ruts and broken rock the Land Cruiser goes bouncing over, but before long I'm beginning to suspect this thing could drive right up the side of the canyon. At one point a coyote pokes its head out from behind a tumbled slab up ahead and peers up and down the trail. I point, to make sure Nat sees it. "He's smarter than you think," he says. "Even the dogs around here know how to cross the street. Maybe something about the desert brings out their survival skills." I wonder if this is true for people too. A moment later the coyote steps out ten feet in front of us and Nat jams on the brake so hard that maps, water bottles, and binoculars go skidding off the seat onto the floor.

Our destination, which requires a moderate hike beyond the end of the road, is a part of the canyon where the river loops back and forth and nearly meets itself. From above I'm struck by the vast amount of work it's done to progress such a little way, almost like a fencing match between river and rock, a dance of thrusting and parrying.

Nat tells me this type of serpentine river course is called a meander, and when it's dug deep into the rock it's an entrenched meander. I love this name. I decide that if I ever own a country estate, instead of some sleepy name like Foxwood Manor or Crabtree Hollow, I'm going to call it Entrenched Meander. I turn to Nat to propose this plan, but he's staring at a family on their way past us, a young couple in shorts and hiking boots with a little girl between them. The girl, who is three or four, has grabbed her parents' hands and picked up her feet, swinging like a picnic basket between them.

Nat's head swivels all the way around to watch them go, and even after they pass from view he continues to gaze after them. Finally I ask, "Do you know them?"

"No." With what seems a great effort he turns back and continues ahead of me down the trail, more slowly now. "I had a little girl," he says, "about that age." My muscles draw inward and I warily wait to see what's coming next. He sidesteps down a scree-covered slope and then up again over tumbled boulders, while I skid and slide and clamber after him. He glances back to see if I'm still behind him, then adds, "She died of meningitis three years ago."

I stop for a moment, balanced precariously on a tilted slab, and stare at his back, the muscles working under his shirt, keeping him going. It doesn't feel right to go on crunching through the gravel behind him, so I try to step silently, to erase myself. A foot-long lizard appears in our path and crouches there doing pushups as it eyes us, deliberating. Nat watches it and says, "My wife moved to Seattle and went to law school. She couldn't pick up the pieces of her life, so she tried to start a new one. I came down here."

He waits for the lizard to disappear into a crevice, then continues to the overlook just ahead. I try to think of something appropriate to say, while the river slides silently through its maze far below us. A heavily eroded fin juts out between the two loops of the riverbed, the river hurling itself at the attached end, then going around the long way. "Eventually," Nat says, pointing, "the river will wear its way through there. Then it will take the shortcut, and that whole loop of canyon will be abandoned."

This seems almost inconceivable. The loop in question is such a vital part of the whole, so perfectly formed for the channeling of water. I try to imagine it riverless, its majestic curves cradling empty air. I wonder if my father saw this, if he foresaw its fate. "What will happen to it then?" I ask.

He shrugs. "It'll gradually fill with debris. As the canyon erodes, rock will pile up, and there won't be anything to carry it away."

"What a waste," I say faintly.

"Yes."

We walk on to the end of the trail, another overlook with a vast view to the south, canyons inside of canyons and the great river flowing away to keep its appointment with the rest of the world. I follow it through the binoculars as far as I can see, studying every bend, then turn to Nat to offer him a look. But he's gazing down into the bottom of the canyon, his eyes unfocused, and I know that what he's looking at is time.

I've looked at time like that. For four years I thought Colin with his luminous eyes looked at me the way he did because I was so damned wonderful. So I didn't believe him the day he told me it wasn't any good and he was going, nor the next day when he didn't come back. Not until the third day did I realize that special intensity was just the color of his eyes, and what I'd thought for all those years had never happened. That was when I sat on a slab of broken granite with seaworn edges and counted the waves, wondering how many of them would roll across the ocean to smash against the sea wall before I adjusted to this new reality.

We stand looking into the chasm, as others have done for thousands of years before us, allowing the movement of the river to take the place of thought for a few moments, then turn and start back up the trail, a little of the canyon and the river and the silence coming along with us.

We don't have very much to say on the rocky ride back. As we approach the motel, he suggests another outing in a couple of days. This means changing my ticket again, but I agree without hesitation. In the parking lot he gets out of the Land Cruiser, comes around to my side, and puts his arms around me. For a minute we hold each other, and I'm not sure if we're sharing our sense of camaraderie or simply holding each other up.

In the evening the motel room starts threatening me with its emptiness again. My father and Colin are both there in some negative way, like holes in my body, a constant presence to remind me of a constant absence. I think about Nat's wife, wonder if she knew anyone in Seattle or if she started out in a room like this. Hers seems even worse than mine, overfilled with what isn't there, and then it turns into mine, and the next thing I know I'm on my way to the office with the ice bucket again.

Tracy looks up and says, "Did you see that big old full moon out there?"

"Oh. Yes. I mean no. I don't know." She looks at me again and her smile disappears. She reaches under the desk and produces a bottle of tequila. "There's a folding chair behind that door," she says, and she gets two plastic cups out of a drawer and pours. I tell her some of my story, the part about my dad and some of the part about Colin. She shakes her head and murmurs now and then, and finally she says, "All this happens and you're out here looking at rocks? What do you think, you're going to get some sympathy from them? I don't know, Janis, my experience has been the rocks don't care. If it was me, I'd be home with my friends."

I nod and agree that sympathy is in short supply in the desert. And yet there is something about the rocks, something besides their impassive unconcern.

When the tequila makes me sleepy enough I get up and thank her for the tea and sympathy, and she says, "Some tea," and I realize she's never heard of that play, but it doesn't matter. I cross back over to my room as the nearly full moon settles on top of the Moab Rim.

Balanced Rock: A structure created when a harder upper layer of rock erodes more slowly than the softer layer beneath it. The formation, which occurs only rarely, requires uniform erosion on all sides of the softer layer to create a pedestal. This structure enjoys only a brief life in geological terms, as continued erosion eventually causes all balanced rocks to topple.

By the time Nat is due again I've acquired some bona fide hiking boots that I'm eager to show off, and have collected a list of new things I've seen—petroglyphs and ripple rock and a hanging garden of ferns and columbine—that I'd like to show him. I've washed my jeans and my hair, and I'm feeling pretty good when I step outside to wait.

After a half hour I'm feeling a little less good, and after an hour I'm not feeling very good at all. When the Land Cruiser finally rolls into the lot and Nat climbs out, I promptly forget my annoyance. He's haggard and pale, hollows under his eyes, his shoulders at an odd angle. "For heaven's sake," I say, "what's happened?"

He shakes his head. "I don't think it's going to work out today. I've had a really rough night."

"So I see. Did you eat something funny?"

"No, nothing like that. Just thoughts. They still win sometimes."

"I'm . . . really sorry," I say, feeling useless, wondering if sympathy can make any difference. He nods and says, "I think I'd better go on home," and I think home for him must seem about like my motel room just now. I watch as he pulls back onto the highway, starting to raise my hand as if to wave but dropping it again. The Land Cruiser shrinks to a smaller and smaller square of blue as it follows the Moab Rim south, and I wonder if he finds its mass as comforting as the Book Cliffs or if he's cursing its implacable indifference.

I get in my car and turn south toward the Needles. The morning is already hot. The Weather Channel, which has been keeping me company at night, has been warning of a heat wave spreading across the area. Nat's grief, or mine, or maybe my father's, drifts in and out of the car like the snatches of cloud that pass now and then in front of the blazing sun.

The Needles resemble a forest of battered and eroded orange spires, or a great city half demolished by war, except that here the battle is still going on, and the wreckage is magnificent. It would be difficult to imagine a landscape more different from the gentle hills of southern New Hampshire, the landscape of my childhood, where my mother took me one day when I was five to watch my father at work. The crew was putting roads into a new tract development. We stood on a knoll and watched him perched up on the steam roller, his burly arms working the controls. The checkerboard of straight roads and square corners reminded me of the rows of thick rubber bands around the box of documents he kept on the closet shelf. I'd asked him why so many rubber bands, and he'd said to keep the papers safe. It seemed to me that was what he was doing there too, rolling out strong glossy black bands that held the earth together, kept the rolling hills in place. But nothing is safe in the Needles.

I leave the car near a trailhead and strap on my pack. As the trail descends, the spires along the horizon slowly disappear from view, one band or groove at a time, but from the bottom up, the opposite of what nature has planned. A jay squawks from a clump of pinyon pines nearby, its blue brilliant against the orange rock face. Beyond it, in an indentation halfway down the canyon wall, invisible in the shadow until I look right at it, is an Anasazi ruin, the half-tumbled walls of an ancient cliff dwelling, slowly untelling its story as it disintegrates.

The trail follows a wide bench for awhile, cliffs rising up steeply on one side and plunging downward on the other, the relentless push of rock and pull of empty space making me feel off balance. There's no shade here, and the heat is intense. When I tip my head back to drink, I make a discovery: high on the canyon wall are petroglyphs, etchings of hands and feet with varying numbers of fingers and toes, torsos with square shoulders and narrow waists. The concerns of a thousand years ago, preserved in the impermanent rock

The trail becomes more difficult, twisting through fallen rock and narrow spaces and along steep and barren slopes. I'm so intent on my search for handholds and footholds that I'm surprised when I suddenly find myself in the creek bed on the canyon floor. Surrounding me are cottonwood and tamarisk, grasses of many sorts, evening primrose everywhere—a veritable Eden. The creek itself is not much more than a trickle right now, though the broad bed of rock and grit betrays the torrent that surges through at other times.

I turn into a side canyon and soon come upon a series of fins splayed from the side of a mesa like a row of disused drive-in movie screens. They tower over the rubble scattered below, the sky intensely blue overhead. A wisp of cloud passes across the sun, and its shadow flickers over each fin in its turn, each with its own surface features and pattern of colors. The shapes lend themselves to imaginary scenes.

Like Colin's eyes, they give back only what I bring to them: the rumpled sweep of empty ocean, a sagging fence on a windswept plain. Strange creatures borne away on mournful wings.

Or maybe that one is Nat's vision. I imagine what my father must have seen: battered villages, blasted trees, felled comrades, hands and feet and torsos—images I've borrowed from other wars and pasted onto his, images once hidden in the hectic tangle of the jungle and now laid bare on the red, red rock under a relentless sun. The air shimmers in the heat and the surface seems to crumble before my eyes. Mesas shrink to buttes, to spires, to boulders, pebbles, sand. The images are carried away by the river, absorbed by cottonwood and tamarisk, lapped by coyote, jay, and bobcat, swept into the sea.

When I begin the climb back out, the sun is sinking toward the rim. I'm powdered with red dust from my hair to my boots, remnants of a thousand images clinging for just a little longer.

I stop at the motel office when I return, no ice bucket this time, and tell Tracy I'm checking out in the morning. "Back to civilization, right?" she says. "Have you had enough of our rocks?"

"Well." I settle my bill and thank her for all her help, wishing her good luck with her troubles. She wishes me the same.

Once in my room I'm too tired to notice the bedspread or the cigarette burn. I take the postcard with the picture of the motel on it out of the dresser drawer and write a note to Nat, putting my home address up in the corner, and drop it in the mailbox out front. Then I fall promptly into a deep sleep.

In the morning I pull onto the highway not long after sunup, following the river back along the same route where I first entered this landscape. The walls are low here, but deep in shadow; and the dark water moves swiftly along the canyon bottom toward the frayed and fractured and splendid country downriver, almost as if it knows it has work to do.

* * *

Patricia Hackbarth is a free-lance French horn player who lives and works in New York City. Her stories have appeared or are forthcoming in The Georgia Review, The North American Review, The Nebraska Review, The North Dakota Quarterly, and Literal Latte. Her first novel is being circulated by her agent while she continues work on her second.

Doug Frelke

Waking up

from Harvard Review

———————————— • ————————————

I wake up in a rest area, somewhere between Maine and New York. I am wearing my sweatshirt; at some point, I must have decided on no more cold-chest driving. The sweatshirt smells of old sweat; I have it pulled up over my nose to keep the air warm while I breathe. I pull it down, straighten it across my shoulders. I try to force my eyes wide open, pop them open, as if that will be the proper magic to jumpstart me.

The sun fills the whole windshield, floods in through the side windows, reflects off the mirrors like steel beams crossing the blue plastic seat. I was dreaming of sleep—the real kind, like when you are a kid, and worn out from kid things, like climbing trees and throwing rocks. My dream had a specific place, the beach at Fort Macon, me falling asleep on an old Indian blanket next to my mother, her voice scolding lightly. Sand in my hair, the salty, swollen taste of my own tongue.

And then awake, like rusty sticks and cold, but at least my head is clear—delicate, but clear. My stomach hurts though, cramps from the Antabuse.

A policeman taps on the Duster's passenger window.

I shield my eyes. He crosses over to the driver's side. I roll down my window, slowly, using two hands.

"The window sticks, officer," I say.

"Can you get out of the car, sir?" I notice that his hand is on his gun.

"Sure." I keep my hands open, out in front of me. When I get out of the car, I raise them over my head slightly.

"You can put your hands down, sir."

I notice that I am parked on the grass. I have driven through the gravel at the end of the parking lot and up onto the dogwalk grass—maybe ten feet or so. The ground is frozen; still, I have managed to cut black strips of mud into the grass.

"May I see your license and registration?"

"Sure." Stupidly, I give him my whole wallet. I bend back into the car for the registration. I feel lightheaded then, bending, and have to catch myself on the steering wheel.

"Are you a veteran?"

The cop has flipped open the wallet. My military I.D. and my driver's license are right in the front, under plastic on opposite sides.

"Yeah."

"When did you get out?"

"Two years ago. Right after Desert Storm."

"You were in the War?"

"Yes I was, officer." I relax. I was in the War. I was, actually, technically, a war hero. My minesweeper, the USS *Fearless*, swept twenty-eight mines off the coast of Kuwait. We were even in the Portland paper when I got back. I received the Navy Commendation Medal with a "V" for valor. The newspaper clipping is in the wallet too, and I show the cop the old, yellowed page. He holds it gingerly, pointing the fading print towards the sun.

"My captain got the bronze star and the crew got a meritorious unit commendation."

The policeman hands me back the clipping, my wallet, the registration. "Are you sober?"

"Yes, sir." I look at my watch; there is hardened dirt on the face. I had left around four yesterday; it is now ten a.m. "I haven't had anything to drink since 1600 yesterday."

The cop looks at me; there is more mud on my pant leg around the knee. "I don't have any alcohol in the car, and I have about three or four dollars on me. I'm heading south, going back home. That's where I'm from." Then I force my mouth shut, and wait for him to render some kind of judgment.

The cop's blue eyes take in the car, then me, the rest area, then me, then he stares off into the woods behind the rest room. He takes off his hat, brushes his hand over his close-cropped black hair. "Would you like some breakfast?" he says.

* * *

I was wrong about my location—I am in New Jersey, and I follow the cop to a diner, called The Garden State. I was nervous that I wouldn't be able to eat, and that that would disappoint him or convince him I was a true hard-line case, with my stomach all but gone. Soon as we walk in, though, I am fine. I smell bacon and coffee and melting butter, and I am ready to eat. He orders piles of waffles and country-fried steak and white gravy biscuits and I am shoveling it all in, drinking coffee and grapefruit juice. I feel a raving kind of hunger, just like after a hard ride off Hatteras when the seasickness finally passed.

He tells me his favorite uncle was killed in Vietnam.

"I was only seven. He was twenty-two. He'd always bring me things—toys my mom thought I was too young for—he gave me a great model of an F-4 phantom. And I put the whole thing together, didn't screw up a thing. I still have it."

I nod, slurping my coffee. "Vietnam was different. What they did was a lot harder than what I did." Which is what I really think. I am ashamed to be around Vietnam vets; and I gave them a wide berth at the Portland VA. They are missing body parts, missing huge chunks of their psyche. And I imagine that their hoary eyes would see me as an elaborate, polished fake, their vision so much more piercing than the social workers' or the psychiatrists'.

"I lost one buddy; when we got back. He made it all through the war and got killed in a driveby in

Charleston." I cut a piece of steak, way too large, and shove the whole thing in my mouth. "That's ironic, huh?"

The cop wrinkles his face. I am ruining the story for him. He knows about driveby shootings and irony. He has seen that, probably every day since he was a rookie, and it is one of the things he would tell other people, part of his story about being a cop. He wants me to be his uncle, be like his uncle. Be at least enough to give him my war story. Instead I say, "I bet he'd be proud of you, being a cop. That's a hard job."

He smiles. "Yeah. He wanted to be a cop. When he got back." He is happy now, his blue eyes jet over the road outside the diner, watching. He is readying to leave, to get back to that road and the other roads where his job is. He surprises me a little; he is wise enough to know he should leave while he has what he wants from me.

"This should cover breakfast," he says, laying two twenties on the table.

I nod. "Thanks," I say.

"You be careful," the cop says.

"You too," I say.

He likes that. He puts his hat on. "I will be. Hope you make it home."

"I will. This should get me through." I outline the table of food with my fork. "Thanks," I say.

Then the cop leaves. The waitress brings me fresh coffee, and I ask for some change. I go to the bathroom and wash my face, drying it with paper towels. I buy a pack of Marlboros from the machine near the phone. I sit down to drink my fresh coffee, smoke a cigarette. I lay out a five-buck tip.

A whole new crew of people has filled the diner, rotated in while I was in the bathroom. I think that I am new to them—clean-faced, no more bleary-eyed than any commuter or long-distance trucker. I am nothing different to them, just a face, a plain, invisible, unknown face, and that makes me feel good, to think that it is so easy to start

again, to reset and begin something new, somewhere new. And I am ready to move, to roll, to go home. And for the first time in a long time, I feel that I can make it.

* * *

***Doug Frelke** has been a writer for twelve years. He served in the U.S. Navy for five years. He participated in the Persian Gulf War as an officer on the minesweeper the USS Leader. Doug studied at Temple University before earning his Master of Liberal Arts from Harvard as the first graduate of their Creative Writing Program. He is a member of the Cambridge writing group, the Half-breeds. His work has appeared in the* Harvard Review.

Heidi Shayla

The Coffin Builder's Romance

from Mississippi Review Online

———————————— • ————————————

M y Susannah came to me because Old Man Whipert got downhill of a log deck that rolled right over the top of him and smashed him, *muerto*. Dead. His widow, Lorna, asked me to build his coffin and she brought her cousin Susannah with her, like an angel hovering over her shoulder. My mother used to say that angels follow in the footsteps of dead men. We can feel them brushing past us if we are still and quiet. But when my Susannah came to me with the Widow Whipert, my heart began to beat so hard that I could hear nothing but its drumming in my chest.

Old Man Whipert was Lorna's most recent husband. She was forever marrying old men—men older than her father, men sometimes older than her grandfather. Already she'd outlived five husbands—Old Man Johnson, Old Man Shrewn, Old Man Torin, Old Man Smith, and now Old Man Whipert. And for Old Man Whipert, she wanted a coffin of solid maple. I thought she might want pine, him being just a number five and all, but her eyes were swollen and red from crying and she kept twisting wads of damp Kleenex round and round between her fingers. She insisted that it must be maple, no matter what. Also to remember that he mustn't be cramped at the head or feet because he'd always hated a bed too short, him being a tall man and an equally tall corpse— although now significantly flatter, thanks to that log deck.

"Coffin Man," Lorna said to me. "I don't want him going

into the hereafter with his legs bent; he had bad knees as it was. Do you understand, Coffin Man?"

"I have a name," I wanted to say to her. Not that you'd be likely to hear it, but I do have one and sometimes I say it to myself just to remember that it is mine. I have to say it to myself because, since my good mother died years ago, no one else has called me by it, not even my brother the gravedigger. Everyone else calls me Coffin Man, like the Widow Whipert when she came to order the box for her husband, because I am the *ataudero*, the coffin maker.

"Hey, Coffin Man," they say to me at the market, for instance. "Hey, Coffin Man, will it be your usual two pounds of coffee today?" And I nod and say, "*Sí*. Just coffee."

It is that way when you are the coffin builder. I am not sure why; it is not like I handle bodies. I wouldn't touch a dead man for love or money. Once you step into that line of work, you can't ever wash your hands clean again. I did know a mortician once who could make folks look better dead than they ever had alive; he was a real artist, that one. But I'd look at his hands and think how the scent of the dead and all the chemicals he used must linger on his skin, no matter how much he scrubbed them. My hands, they just smell of the wood and the linseed oil I rub into my coffins.

If it weren't for the fact that I'm a man who craves companionship, coffin building would be the perfect work. There is real skill in it. I've got to joint them together just so and I only use true dovetails or mortise and tenons. I have to sand them to a fine finish and the wood must be oiled or varnished, and finally the coffins are padded with satin or velvet so the dead look as comfortable as possible leaving this world. My brother, he's happy just making his money digging a hole and going home; there's no pride in it for him. But me, I'm an artisan. I wouldn't want a person to head into the afterlife in a shoddy coffin. I make them to last longer than the bones inside.

But it is solitary work. My brother's not much of a talker,

so it doesn't bother him. But me, I can't get enough of talking back and forth, noticing the weather, gossiping, arguing—in Spanish or in English, it makes no difference to me; I appreciate a little human contact. I used to go to the bar for a beer, to surround myself with human voices. There is only one bar but inside there are three groups. The Mexican mill workers and choker setters sit together behind the pool tables. The Anglos sit at the long wooden bar on red stools. And the timber fallers, catskinners, and toppers—Mexicans and whites—play pool together all night long. The bartender goes back and forth between them. I used to sit in the middle, by myself.

The men would all be over-polite and distant with me, but it was enough to just sit amongst them and listen. Afterwards, on my way home, I would say out loud what I would have said at the bar, if I had been allowed into the conversations I overheard. In the dark of my car, I argued, agreed, laughed, told jokes and riddles, ordered a round for the house, and imagined friends slapping me on the back in thanks. It wasn't perfect, but at least it was better than the silence of my brother, the gravedigger.

One night Jonas Tico sat down on the barchair next to me. He staggered around the pool tables with a glass of whisky in his hand, pushing people out of his way, steering himself roughly in my direction. When he managed to slide himself onto the stool, I could see that he had somehow missed his mouth taking a drink and whisky was running down his big black beard and dripping onto his shirtfront.

Jonas was a drunk, but only at night. During the day he was a timber faller who was known to lay a Douglas Fir down in a line so straight and precise two men could stand on either side of it and the tree would just blow their hair as it fell between them. Jonas had one other talent as well; he had a remarkable ability to defy death, even though it tried to snare him constantly.

That year alone he had survived two near fatal incidents. First he stumbled into the middle of somebody's pot patch and was shot in the stomach. He went to the hospital with his intestines looped over his arm to keep them from falling out entirely onto the floorboard of his brother's pickup. Then that summer he fell out of a tree two hundred feet above the river and belly flopped onto the water so hard it collapsed one of his lungs and broke his collarbone. Some sunbathers down river at the nude swimming hole saved him when he floated past. Jonas said he woke up surrounded by breasts and asses. He thought for sure he'd died, but he couldn't decide if he'd gone to heaven or hell, depending on which piece of anatomy was facing him at any given moment.

Jonas was definitely drunk when he sat down next to me at the bar. He leaned in close to my face, so I could see the droplets of whisky dripping off his beard. "How many board feet will it take for me, Coffin Man?" he asked. "How big a box will it take to bury me in?"

I left without answering Jonas's question, knowing for a fact that, as much as I pined for a human voice and a touch, there'd be no going back to the bar. I was like a ghost whispering to people when they least expected it. I made them look at dying. I got into my car and drove toward home. I found myself crying as I drove and I wondered if the tears were for the people at the bar or for myself, but I couldn't decide the answer.

After that, I kept to my wood shop where I built my coffins and had conversations now and then with the morticians who placed their orders with me; we talked of wood and dimensions. Sometimes widows, like Lorna, would come to my shop to order coffins for husbands who had been killed in the woods or the mills, but then there was sobbing and only more talk of wood and dimensions. It was a solitary life for a man like me.

I was thinking about that as I wrote up the order for Old Man Whipert's coffin. Lorna was sitting on my stool, crying and twisting her Kleenex between her hands, demanding maple, and that the coffin mustn't be too small, and that it must be built to last forever. It occurred to me that, since a goodly number of Old Man Whipert's bones had been crushed by the logs that killed him, there was no doubt that the wood would outlast him; when there was nothing left of him but powder, my coffin would still be there, cradling the dust of his broken bones.

So as the Widow Whipert went on, I concentrated instead on her cousin, Susannah. Susannah split her time between holding Lorna's hands, and looking over my arm at the order sheet. "It costs a lot to bury a man," she said.

I nodded, "It does if you're doing it in maple. More yet if you want walnut or oak."

"Oh, but it must be maple," wailed the Widow Whipert. "No matter what the cost."

Susannah confessed secretly to me that she was worried that Lorna was so shocked by the death of number five, she might never get over it. I told Susannah I thought Lorna would find a way to move on; I was thinking that there were two or three more old widowers still available yet.

In fact Lorna brightened considerably when my brother appeared from out back. Her wailing stopped and she suddenly began to dab at her eyes with the mangled Kleenex. "Oh my, I must look just a mess," she said.

My brother, who in the past had always tried to avoid speaking English whenever possible, now took his hat off and said, "*Senora*, I think you look very good, considering the circumstances of your visit."

Lorna smiled and fanned herself with her hand, saying again, "Oh my!"

She jumped right up and pulled him by the arm to her car to talk about the proper length of her number five's grave, so his coffin didn't fit too tight. Things being too small was something the widow seemed overly worried about. My brother let himself be drug away, smiling, while the Widow Whipert talked at him without pause about grave digging and, oh my, what a set of chest and arm muscles it gave him.

That left Susannah the cousin alone to admire the coffins I had in progress. She said she had a particular fondness for boxes, and judging from the breathless way she said it, I had to trust that what she said was so. She ran her hands over the wood and the velvet with such emotion that I had to turn away to contain myself. I went to work planing a long maple coffin that I had begun several days earlier to fill an order for a mortuary in town. Now the mortuary would have to wait because the long maple coffin was going to become Old Man Whipert's final resting place. The plane dropped curls of wood shavings behind it onto the floor at my feet.

Susannah pulled up my tall stool and perched herself there to watch me work. Whenever I turned my head, I could see her bare legs swinging from beneath her sundress, stirring the wood dust beneath the stool. Her legs were a distracting sight. And then she began to talk to me. We talked of the weather and Lorna's deceased husbands. We spoke of wood and oils and varnishes. She asked me how I became a coffin builder and I found myself telling her, and reveling in the wonder of sitting in my woodshop having a conversation with a woman in a sundress and bare legs.

"I didn't exactly aspire to become a coffin builder," I told her. "But it is what I became because my father— rest his soul—was a stone carver. He learned from his father in Mexico when he was a boy. And his father had learned from his father. In Mexico, my family were all stone carvers. My father said our ancestors were enslaved and put to work in the silver mines by the *Conquistadores.* The story says that so many of them died in the *Conquistadores'* mines, our blood began to run gray and black, the color of stone. That is what my father said and why all the men in my family for generations were stone carvers—because it was in their blood.

"After my father came here, he carved gravestones on weekends for extra cash. He had a delicate hand with the lettering and could do a fine pair of angel's wings or a lovely cross for a bit more money. He always did baby's headstones for less and he would carve a sweet lamb into the stone for no extra charge. Otherwise, it was so much a letter and a bit more for wings or crosses. He always said that carving headstones was sure work; everybody had to die sooner or later and you could count on making a little cash off of those who went before you, if you were any kind of a hand at carving stones."

Susannah kicked off her sandals and stretched her legs down to run her feet through the pile of wood shavings I had made with the planer. She pushed them against my boots and let her toes trail across my pants leg. "Then why aren't you a stone carver, Coffin Man?" she asked softly.

"Well," I swallowed, "neither my brother or I had the patience for it. We broke more good pieces of marble trying to develop the knack than I care to remember. My father always said we were the end of a proud line of carvers. But he insisted that, since he had made it a tradition round about for our family to be involved in the laying to rest of the dearly departed, and because it was sure work, we had to find our place in the business. He said everyone has to die sooner or later, and they'll likely need a good box to be buried in."

I stopped planing and knit my eyebrows together to look like my father. "'Since you can't carve a stone to save your soul,' he'd say, 'the next best thing is building coffins.'"

I shrugged my shoulders at Susannah, "So I became a coffin builder."

"It is good work," Susannah said. "My father always told me that a man is as close to God as he can get when he works with the harvest of the earth." And then she laughed, "But he also said that a man was as close to God as he could get when he was inside a woman, so it is hard to tell which thing was the more holy."

I cleared my throat and began to sand the coffin, thinking that her father must have been a smart man, although right then, with Susannah's bare legs swinging in front of me, I didn't think there was any question about which activity I would choose. I asked about her fondness for boxes in order to change the subject.

She told me she had hundreds of boxes from all over the world—all sizes and shapes and colors.

"What do you do with them all?" I asked her, "Where do you keep them?"

She got that breathy voice again. "I keep them all over my house," she said. "Everywhere." And then she laughed and kicked her legs some more. "Boxes excite me, Coffin Man. Every woman loves a good box."

That left me thinking about boxes, and being inside a woman, and bare legs, and her breathy excited voice. I nearly sanded right over the top of my fingers.

By the time Lorna and my brother appeared, Susannah was on her knees beside me with a piece of sandpaper helping to smooth the corners of Old Man Whipert's coffin. We were talking about the lining that would go inside, about velvet and satin and what it must feel like to lie down on such fabrics naked. When Lorna saw her cousin sanding on the coffin, she began to dab at her eyes again with the Kleenex and Susannah had to lead her away to the car. I promised that the coffin would be done in two days, in time for the funeral, although it would mean staying up half the night to finish it.

My brother and I watched the women drive away, and I thought I saw the same look of wonderment on his face as I felt on my own. I wondered then how I would ever be the same, having sanded wood with a woman like Susannah, who loved boxes.

* * *

Susannah came to pick up Old Man Whipert's coffin because Lorna was busy overseeing the digging of his grave. Already Lorna and my brother had been at the graveyard for two days—him digging and her offering comments on the size of the hole and of his arms and chest. It seemed to me that my brother was taking an inordinate amount of time to dig a grave that would normally have taken him just a few hours.

Susannah helped me load the coffin in the back of Old Man Whipert's pickup and then she perched herself on my stool again and began to swing her legs, which made me have to sit down also. "Do you sew the satin and the velvet for the linings yourself?" she asked me.

I nodded, trying not to stare at her legs, "My mother was a seamstress; she taught me to sew. But it's mostly glue with coffin liners."

Susannah smiled, "I would like you to come to my house, Coffin Man. I want to show you my boxes and there are some people I want you to meet."

I wondered what this had to do with coffin liners but my father had always said to not ask questions if you're not sure you want to know the answers.

Instead I told her, "I am not sure, Susannah, that that would be the best thing to do. I make other people nervous. Your friends might not want to be with me."

But Susannah just smiled and slid off my stool, which made her skirt hike up and showed her thigh. "Don't worry, Coffin Man. Just come to my house on Saturday and bring some of your velvet and satin, all right?"

I could not have said no with the memory of her white thigh clouding my thoughts and emotions. "All right then, I'll come," I told her.

"Good," she said, and gathered her things to go. But at the door she turned back and asked, "What is your name?"

I stared at her, silent, shocked at the question for so long that finally she said, "I'm sorry, I shouldn't have asked."

"No, no. I want to tell you. My name ... My name is Gabriel Miguel Raphael." It sounded strange in my own ears hearing it out loud.

Susannah smiled again. "Gabriel, Michael, and Raphael," she said. "The three angels from the Bible."

"It was my mother's idea," I answered. "My father said it was not manly enough."

"It is a good name, Gabriel. Man enough, I think," she said. And then she turned and left, leaving her voice echoing my name through the woodshop.

* * *

My brother the gravedigger attended Old Man Whipert's funeral. When he returned, I asked him about it and he said, "Lorna looks very good in black." I told him that I was going to Susannah's house on Saturday and he raised his eyebrows, but that was all.

* * *

When Saturday came, I spent some time trying to decide what to wear before I gave it up and decided all I had were jeans and work shirts anyway. I bundled up rolls of velvet and satin in reds, blues, purples, greens, and browns. I touched them and remembered the way that Susannah had stroked the cloth and how she had knelt beside me to sand the wood. It made me breathe faster to think of it, of her hands coated in linseed oil and wood dust.

Her house was like a little box in itself, pressed on all sides by trees. She stepped out onto the porch to welcome me and I filled her arms with the bolts of cloth. The material draped off the rolls and I swept the hanging folds up over her shoulders so that she was covered in the velvet and satin. Susannah threw back her head and laughed. "No one has ever wrapped me in velvet before, Gabriel."

Her house was cool and dark inside, shaded by the trees. And everywhere I looked—on shelves, on the floor, on the counter, behind chairs—were boxes. Outside the window, were window boxes full of flowers. Beside the woodstove were boxes of matches, kindling, newspaper, wood. In the kitchen were big plastic boxes full of flour, rice, cornmeal.

In corners and hidden places, she kept small tin boxes full of special things.

She put down the bolts of fabric and led me through the little rooms of her house. We opened boxes and looked inside. We found a long box full of wooden nesting dolls. They were carefully painted with bright red dresses and little shoes. Each identical round figure got smaller and smaller as we split them open to see the brightly painted faces of the ones inside, until we came to the smallest. It was no bigger than a thimble. In a wooden box in the kitchen, I looked at jars of spices. We set them on the windowsill where the sun glinted on the glass and the mix of colors was wondrous—mustard yellow, chile red, nutmeg brown, basil green, turmeric orange. When we came upon a box full of coins, I added a *peso* I had been carrying in my pocket since my father died. And when we found a round hatbox full of polished stones, Susannah chose one that was as brown as wood and gave it to me to fill the spot in my pocket where the *peso* had been.

Next to her bed was a beautiful carved box that was padlocked. I asked her why and she smiled. "I keep my toys in that box, Gabriel."

"Toys?" I asked.

"Yes," she answered, "but not toys for children." She looked at me meaningfully and in that breathy way she had, she said, "It is a special box, Gabriel."

I swallowed several times and blushed, finally understanding what she was saying, and not saying. "*Sí*," was all I could muster myself to answer, which made her laugh.

"Come," she said. "The women will be arriving soon."

"The women?" I asked. But she just led the way back to the living room, where she began to lay out the velvet and satin side by side, holding the colors against each other and shifting them around.

When the other women came, they all brought fabric of their own, and uncompleted quilt blocks, and needles, and thread. They also brought beer and wine. They smiled at me when they came in, all of them, as if I were just another of the women. "This is Gabriel Miguel Raphael," Susannah told them. "He has come to sew with us." They opened the beer and someone handed me a bottle. "Come, Coffin Man," they said. "Come sew."

"Please," I answered. "Please, call me Gabriel. It is my name." I wondered how I was able to say it and knew, even as I wondered, that in Susannah's house, everything was in its place, even me.

The women sat around Susannah's living room and pulled out their quilt blocks. They sewed, talked, laughed, and drank. Susannah gave me yards of the velvet and satin. She sat next to me and we cut diamond shapes until there were piles of them around us. I held the beer bottle between my thighs and felt the warmth of Susannah's leg next to mine. "What are we making?" I asked her.

The women laughed at me. One of them said, "We are making quilts, Coffin Man." And then the others scolded her and said, "His name is Gabriel." They told me about the quilts they were sewing, how the cloth came from a mother's apron, or a child's blanket, or a husband's work shirt, how they were cutting and piecing them into beautiful patterns for their beds or the beds of their families. "Look, Gabriel," they said. "This pattern is called the Drunkard's Path." Or the Lone Star. Or Tumbling Blocks. Or Wedding Ring. Log Cabin. Texas Star. Double Chain. Bear Paw. Turkey Track. Nine Square. "Look, Gabriel," they said. Until my name was ringing in my own ears and Susannah was smiling quietly beside me.

* * *

The quilters met at Susannah's little house once a week. They always brought beer, wine, and their material. In her living room, I learned about their children and husbands. About who was born and who was married. About these women who pieced their lives together in quilts, making scraps into warm thick blankets. Susannah and I stitched the velvet and satin pieces together into larger blocks. We never stopped sewing as we talked.

"Why did you let me into the quilter's group?" I asked the women, "Why is it that you are not nervous with me?"

"What is there to be afraid of you?" they shrugged. "When something dies, there are always pieces of it left behind that can be made into something else—memories, heirlooms, remnants to sew together into something new. What is there to fear?"

They smiled and nodded, making me see that they had nothing to fear from death because its only power was to re-create, an act they understood in their bones. This was the logic of quilters.

* * *

I saw Susannah on Saturdays, to sew the quilt made of coffin liner materials. It was like a medicine to go there and with time I began to see it spilling over onto others. At the market one day, just as the leaves on the maple trees were changing and the green of the fir trees stood out brighter than ever, the man who sold me my coffee said, "Will it be the usual two pounds today, Gabriel?" His wife was a quilter. In gratitude I built them new wooden bins for their coffee beans. Susannah came to my woodshop and painted the bins bright colors while I worked on coffins. Since summer was gone, she had traded her sundresses for jeans and sweatshirts, which were now covered in splashes of paint, the colors crisscrossing each other so that she looked like one of the women's quilts, pieced and patched. Always we talked as we worked, filling the woodshop with our voices. My brother looked in sometimes and shook his head at our chatter. Later, on his way out to see the Widow Whipert, he would ask me what Susannah and I were doing. I said we were making boxes together.

It was winter before the coffee bins were done. The rain beat steadily on the roof of my woodshop. The drivers who came to load coffins onto their trucks for the mortuaries in town bent their heads against it and swore at the cold water running inside the collars of their coats. But Susannah and I lit the woodstove in my shop while we worked and looked out the windows at the endless green of the mountains. The soft pounding of the rain stirred with the snapping of the fire and the scrape of my planing and sanding. In the tiny moments between our words, we could hear it all mixing together around the two of us.

We loaded the coffee bins into the bed of my pickup, to deliver to the market. After we had secured them with ropes and covered them with a tarp, Susannah slipped her hand into mine and said, "They are beautiful, Gabriel." I looked at her hand and could find no words, as if her touch had so filled me with wonder that it had pushed out my voice. I could only nod in agreement, but I did not let go of her hand. I pulled her close to me in the pickup seat as I drove and she told me that when we worked together side by side—making boxes, sewing the quilt—it was like foreplay. I asked her if that meant she would unlock the box by her bed for me someday. She said there was time that day, if we hurried at the market.

I have never driven so fast.

* * *

We talk even when we make love. Always we are talking. Susannah says her house is too small to contain all our chatter, but I do not think this is possible. In Susannah's house, everything is in its place.

Our lives have become attached to the seasons. After the winter coffee bins, we finished our quilt in the spring, when it was already too hot to use it. The design is called Tumbling Blocks, but of course Susannah sees it as Tumbling boxes. In the summer we built a box at the end of her bed to keep the quilt until winter. We put the quilt on the bed and made love on top of it because it was too hot to be beneath its warmth. Then we put it in the box and closed the lid on it, and somehow in the process I became installed in Susannah's house as well, as if I too had been folded up and put away. We took the quilt back out when the rains came harder and got cold enough to chill all the way to the bone. In Susannah's bed—now it is our bed—beneath our quilt, we make love and talk, and afterwards we listen to the rain against the roof.

Next summer I will build a woodshop in the trees behind our house. I will put a sign out front that says *El ATAUDERO*, the coffin maker. Susannah says that the sign should say *El CAJERO*, the box maker. We will see. In the meantime, I go to my brother's house, to my old woodshop. He sits there with me sometimes and says nothing, but that is enough. In his silence, I think he is still saying a lot. I asked him one time about the Widow Whipert. He said perhaps he is too young for her.

After next summer is done, Susannah will have our baby. She says that she is a box and when the door opens and the baby comes out, she will be empty. I talk to the baby in her womb and it kicks and moves in answer; I think it is fighting for *palabras*, for words. I am building it a cradle and we are sewing a new quilt. If the child is a boy, we will name him Gabriel. But when I talk to it through the walls of Susannah's womb, I think I hear it whispering that she is a girl. Then we will name her *Madera* Susannah Raphael. *Madera* means wood. And I will say it out loud to her every day, so that it will echo throughout her life—because a name is sometimes all that is left, the only scrap to sew together, when the body has died.

* * *

Heidi Shayla *was born and raised in the Oregon Coast Range, in the heart of logging country. Her fiction has appeared in the* Mississippi Review, South

Dakota Review, Iron Horse Literary Review, *and* Writers' Forum, *and has been accepted for publication in an upcoming issue of* Prairie Schooner. *Her creative nonfiction has been published* by Denali Literary Journal, Back Home Magazine *and was anthologized in* WRITING WORK: Writers on Working Class Writing, *published by Bottom Dog Press. She was a 2001 recipient of an Individual Artist's Award sponsored by the Oregon Arts Commission and the National Endowment for the Arts. She received her MFA in Creative Writing from Vermont College.*

George Singleton

Richard Petty Accepts National Book Award

from New Delta Review

———————————— • ————————————

L et me say right now that this couldn't've been done without the support of all the good Hewlett-Packard people. The Intel Pentium III, 550 megaherz with 128 MB RAM done us right. There for a while we thought a 20GB hard drive wouldn't be enough for what we had to say, but hot almighty model 8575 chugged along and took the curves. I'm happy to say that we moved over from the 40x/CDRW/DVD CD-ROM—not that we couldn't've wrote what we wrote without it, but hey—we never felt like we was either too tight or too loose in the curves, or like we didn't flat-out have plenty of get-go when we felt pressure from all the other fine writers who published books this year. It's no secret that modem speeds in actual use may vary, but I got to hand it to the HP people for the way they kept me constant. There weren't no surprises, is what I'm saying.

I'd also like to thank the people at LaserJet Laser Paper for the strong, smooth twenty-four pound white paper that won't curl up and wilt, even at Darlington. We done some high-speed copying, and the ink and toner stayed consistent throughout. The extra weight and brightness always assured crisp text, which is important for resumés, brochures, report covers, newsletters, press releases, and the Great American Novel. 96 brightness can't be beat when it comes to LaserJet 4050 Series Printers, which gave us the ability to go seventeen pages a minute. We liked the 1200-by-1200 dpi resolution, and the fifteen-second start-up time probably kept us in business the same way my pit crew did down in Daytona Beach all those years.

Oh I know I'mo' forget somebody.

I can't say enough about the people at Martin Computer Office Grouping. Our credenza, hutch, two-drawer lateral file, deluxe executive computer desk with return and print tower made it easy as coming down pit row at sixty miles per hour when we set ourselves down to write every morning. We'd just pull our Deluxe Ergonomic Manager's Chair with pneumatic and independently adjustable seat height right up to the desk without even having to think about lumbar support, knee tilt, or durable fabric upholstery. Weavetek 100 percent Olefin put us in a good Dusty Rose 541 pattern that suited what we needed to say about the human condition, plus left us comfortable and dry during those humid summer afternoons of conflict between protagonist and antagonist.

Listen, the Great American Novel don't come all at once, and we'd like to thank the Greencycle Recycled Steno Book people for their high-quality six-by-nine inch green tint, Gregg ruled pads where we took notes and drew charts up about conflict and plot. Let me say to all the aspiring writers out there that I wrecked a good twenty pads before finding the groove on the outside of the home office, I tell you what.

Now I know a lot of the rest of the field went with Uni-Ball Roller Grip pens because of the steel point added strength and resistance to smears, but I got to tell you— towards the end there we just decided to take a chance on Papermate stick pens in black medium. The durable ballpoint tip withstood everyday office use there down the stretch. I can't say for sure I'd've made it another couple chapters, but the team made a decision and stuck to it. For those of y'all not acquainted to the nuances of composition, it's a lot like taking on two Goodyears at the end of the Coca-Cola 600 instead of opting for four.

I ain't too proud to admit that I partook of the *Webster's*

New World Dictionary put out by Simon and Schuster. I ain't too proud to admit that on those cold winter nights when we couldn't even think of a good character's name, I got some support from Jim Beam and Jack Daniels and George Dickel, not necessarily in that order.

We can't forget the Xerox Remanufactured Cartridge people. I don't know how many nights I called them people up and said, "Hey, I need a remanufactured laser printer cartridge pronto up here in North Carolina." They'd work all night long so I wouldn't have to start next day at the back of the pack, which ain't easy. Ask any driver in Rockingham, Richmond, or Pocono.

I remember one time at Bristol when I couldn't keep up with what went on. Back then I could've used a printing calculator with twelve-digit fluorescent display and mark-up/mark-down function. We couldn't've kept up our pace without the AC-powered Canon MP25D, just to let us know where we were in the novel, what with chapters, and scenes, and pages, and sentences. And words. Finally on the hardware front I got to tip my hat to the people at Acco for their smooth, non-skid, regular and jumbo paper clips.

And the people at Brown Kraft Recycled Clasp Envelopes for sending my first chapters off to the agent.

Now I know y'all in attendance might think writing the Great American Novel don't take much more than one idea and a support team like I done mentioned. Somebody famous said once that, "Clothes make the man." Well, that's true. I don't know if I coulda finished up my pivotal climactic scene without the support of the people at authentic Dickies workshirts—another 100 percent cotton product made ovair in Bangladesh. We couldn't finish a minor scene—much less a chapter—without the good work of the people down at Stetson. And Dingo boots. And Ray-ban sunglasses.

And, more than anyone else, we want to thank Mrs. Louise Gowers, who taught me how to type back in high school. F-R-F-R-F-R. J-U-J-U-J-U. Don't look at the keyboard. Ruler on knuckles. A lot of people think it only takes "Once upon a time" or "It was a dark and stormy night" or "Call me (whatever that guy's name was on the boat)," but I'm here to tell you that it all starts with a ruler on knuckles.

* * *

George Singleton's *first collection,* THESE PEOPLE ARE US, *will come out in paperback from Harcourt's Harvest line in the fall of 2002. His second collection of short stories,* THE HALF-MAMMALS OF DIXIE, *will be published by Algonquin in September, 2002. His stories have appeared in* The Atlantic Monthly, Harper's, Book, Playboy, Zoetrope: All-Story, *and in five* NEW STORIES FROM THE SOUTH.

2001 Silver Rose Award Honorable Mentions

Ben Brooks
The Wooden Flute
from The Alaska Quarterly Review

Bobbie Ann Mason
Three-Wheeler
from The Atlantic Monthly

Jason Schossler
Offerings
from The Indiana Review

About The Editors

Kevin Watson *serves on the board of the Salem College Center for Women Writers. His short stories have appeared in* ART Ideas Magazine, Amarillo Bay, The Incunabula, The Rose and Thorn Literary E-zine, *and others. His short story* Sunny Side Up *won first prize in the 2002 OutRider Press/TallGrass Writers Guild short fiction contest and will appear in the 2002 anthology TAKE TWO—THEY'RE SMALL. His short story* Some Kind Of Romantic *was awarded the 2002 Katherine B. Rondthaler Award for Prose.*

Writer-lecturer **Alexandra York** *is an internationally published author of books, magazine and newspaper articles, essays, book and movie reviews, short stories, song lyrics and poetry. She founded and is president of American Renaissance for the Twenty-first Century (ART), a nonprofit educational arts foundation devoted to a rebirth of beauty and life-affirming values in all of the fine arts and was Editor of its magazine,* ART Ideas. *She received the 1997 Whiting Memorial Award for outstanding service to the cultural world from the International Society for Philosophical Enquiry. She is listed in* Who's Who of American Women *and* Who's Who in America. *Her latest book is* FROM THE FOUNTAINHEAD TO THE FUTURE and Other Essays on Art and Excellence.

ART
AMERICAN RENAISSANCE FOR
THE TWENTY-FIRST CENTURY

is a 501(c)(3) nonprofit educational foundation dedicated to a rebirth of beauty and life-affirming values in all of the fine arts.

For more information, including membership, contact:
ART, FDR Station, P.O. Box 8379, New York, NY 10150-1919.
Phone: (212) 759-7765, FAX: (212) 759-1922
All donations are fully tax deductible as provided by law.

Other publications include:

FROM THE FOUNTAINHEAD TO THE FUTURE and Other Essays on Art and Excellence, by Alexandra York ($14)

Four-color artist catalogues:
ROMANTIC REALISM: Visions of Values, featuring title essay and thirteen painters and sculptors ($10)

THE LEGACY LIVES: The World at its Most Beautiful and Man and Woman at their Best, featuring title essay and thirty-five painters and sculptors ($20)

ART Ideas magazine: Back issues ($5 each)

Add $2 for Shipping and handling to all publications except ART Ideas (S&H included) for U.S. Please contact ART for information regarding shipping overseas.

TEMPLE OF TRIUMPH posters:

Signed by architect, sculptor, poet and composer ($100)
Unsigned ($50), (Add $3 S&H for U.S.)

Send checks (sorry, no credit cards) to ART at the above address.

PLEASE BE INVITED TO VIEW ALL OF THE ABOVE OFFERINGS ON ART'S WEB SITE: www.ART-21.org